SEX: FROM THE COUCH

SEX: FROM THE COUCH

Dr. Arlene G. Krieger

These Non-fiction stories reveal true experiences of life, love and relationships. The author has disguised the identities of all, and in some instances created composite characters, however none of the changes have affected the truthfulness, quality and accuracy of the significance of the stories. Although the author and publisher have made every effort to ensure that the information in this book was correct at press time, the author and publisher do not assume and hereby disclaim any liability to any party for any loss, damage, or disruption caused by errors or omissions, whether such errors or omissions result from negligence, accident, or any other cause.

Identifiers: LCCN: 2018903545
Copyright Certificate of Registration: TXu 2-036-607
ISBN-13: 978-1484076576
ISBN-10: 1484076575

Jacket Image: Shutterstock
Publisher: The BlueBird Books
Edited by: eliteauthors.com

Dedicated, in loving memory, to my departed father, a WWII navy pilot, who taught me to live my life with an everlasting tenacity and passion for life. To my children, now all exceptional adults, a special thank-you for being you.

Love always begets more love in this world.

Dr. Arlene Krieger

CONTENTS

Litany

You are the bread and the knife,
the crystal goblet and the wine...

—Jacques Crickillon

You are the dew on the morning grass and the
burning wheel of the sun. You are the white apron
of the baker, and the marsh birds suddenly in flight.

However, you are not the wind in the orchard, the
plums on the counter, or the house of cards. And
you are certainly not the pine-scented air. There is
just no way that you are the pine-scented air ...

—Billy Collins

Deliciously twisted…The best collection of human stories to date. Your experiences of love and life would be poorer without it. Written from a sexologist's observations and views on the birth and death of relationships, these thirteen exquisite tales give us the often tragic, romantic, sexy realms of what really happens behind closed doors. This collection is both dangerously funny and heartbreaking. Does a "living happily ever after" relationship exist? Who makes it? What breaks it? Here you will find the answers, offered up to you for your consideration. Enjoy the journey as you are invited into the reality of the human conditions of love, lust, and relationships.

INTRODUCTION

Sing in me, Muse, and through me tell the story.

—Homer

My narratives come from the heart and from exposure as a seasoned therapist to the rhythmic patterns of love and life. Every story reflects a different journey in life. From my personal perspective as a PhD sexologist, it seems most people are always seeking answers to the eternal questions of why we do what we do to our partners and why we create the things that we impose on each other, all in the name of love? These thirteen tales portray the bizarre, eccentric, erotic, and curious behaviors of all those who are single, dating, or married.

Some have said these accounts are dark without happy endings—I disagree. This amalgamation of bits and pieces of human experience came together as characters in a reflection of life happening between dusk and dawn—often pointless efforts in the name of love. However, we as individuals are always hoping, looking for inspiration, and wanting to believe in love. Whenever

I'm asked if I think that authentic love is possible, I smile sincerely and say, "Yes, just don't take too long with the wrong person if you ever expect to come across it." Statistically, 99 percent of the people you meet will not be a good match for you. Therefore, if you spend a year with each guy/girl you date, you'll require ninety-nine years to meet that right one!

Generally, from listening to people throughout the years, it appears that those who are married are often restless and wish to be free—and the ones who find themselves single, for the most part, eventually want the archetype of marriage. The implied message of an old proverb from the fourteenth century, "a rolling stone gathers no moss," refers to a wanderer or those who want to be free.

I frequently think of this prophetic quote when dealing with individuals and couples whose relationships have grown old and brittle, like ancient, blighted bark found under moss-covered rocks. I'm not speaking of *old* as in chronological age, but rather the state, condition, and disorder of the relationship. For the most part, many in long-term relationships feel trapped and can only dream of the "promised land," of some idea that they have in their minds, an image of something better, sexier, and more exciting—only ultimately to find that the grass isn't always greener on the other side.

So, primarily in the relationship-age population there are those who decide to couple up, and there are likewise those who stay single—maintaining their sovereignty, claiming to be happy with being the archetypal wandering soul, forever paired to freedom, the perpetual rolling stone. Please keep in mind that the person who opts not to be in a relationship can experience love and lust; however, such person finds themselves in an entirely different universe than that of an exclusive and sole, dedicated love.

We as people, for the most part, are not naturally monogamous beings. We can love many people in a lifetime and love them differently, separately, with great affection and passion—loving them with no rhyme or reason, frequently confusing us beyond imagination, wreaking havoc on all involved. Nevertheless, real love can and does exist. Not for the faint of heart, love entails dedication and commitment, along with the responsibilities that come with this type of devotion in allowing another person into your soul or life energy.

People say they are looking for perfection in a mate. Love, however, is never perfect. It is irrational, passionate, and complicated. But often the passion wanes, and long-term relationships can lack movement, creativity, and curiosity to keep the bond between two people continuously rejuvenated and alive. In this book, you'll explore the folly of humanity and the bizarre inconsistency of what we call love.

The recurring issues and questions of why love becomes boring and stale have always been at the forefront of most relationship problems. What does the term *love* mean in the social context of our time? Rather than write a clinical book on these issues, I composed this book, a free fall of narratives revealing the most obscure and yet cutting themes of love, lust, and relationships.

Not every story here will speak to you because "truth is singular," and its many versions are often mistruths. So, our belief systems, our truths, often become our interpretations of the universe we dwell in and, therefore, our absolutes in reasoning, and decision-making processes— the way in which we develop our position on life. Who is the victim or villain in these vignettes of love and yearning? Willing or innocent, predatory or provocateur, we are all equally part of the human species and want a human connection.

Why can't you stay in love the way it was when you first met? Can you remember that feeling of being so fully alive and happy inside as your heart skipped a beat in receiving your new lover's phone call, text, or e-mail? Just hearing that "ping" set you on fire with hopes and dreams of romance and unbridled desire. Where did all the excitement go? Can those feelings ever come back as strong as in the beginning? For many, sexuality and intimacy within a healthy relationship is still a mysterious, misunderstood, complex problem continuously arising in their relationships and daily interactions.

Whether it is an issue of someone wanting more, wanting something sexually different (or differently exciting), a disappointment, or promises not kept, there it is, the ugly truth that you just aren't attracted to your partner anymore. It can hit you as suddenly as an afternoon thunderstorm—the realization that your feelings for your mate have changed. You find yourself daydreaming or having fantasies about that hard-bodied guy with the come-hither smile who passed by you in the supermarket aisle, or the attractive and mysterious woman who you could swear winked at you in the coffee shop this morning.

What is this thing that we call *love*? Forget about the word *love* for the moment. The essential questions are as follows: What about the relationship and its parameters and expectations? And are you and your mate on the same page? You may find yourself asking, "How the heck did I wind up here? Indeed, is this all there is? Who is this person I'm with? And what have we become?"

These are the questions held closest to the bone, based on our societal and imposed norms, yet, basically spawned by our primordial instincts. Current-day anthropologists still maintain that we as humans are not naturally monogamous, not inherently or genetically exclusive. Of course, then our limbic brains keep urging us to hunt while the amygdala taunts us to mate with all the plentiful choices out there. What if you have committed to a one-on-one relationship? What to do?

Having worked with thousands of people over the years, from all walks and social contexts of life, I can confirm the truth of the figure of speech "love comes in many shapes and sizes." We all love differently. It is not merely one's decision of how to love or even how to befriend another person, but rather a circumstance of how a person's family of origin often informs their capacity to love. These struggles over someone's essential nature and personal history then become integrated into their personality, delineating and hardwiring how they learned to love and ultimately defining how they will be able to love another.

As a doctor and an author, I have spent years learning from life and career experiences, distilling the secrets of what we as human beings accumulate and do to each other in relationships. These glimpses of life, hopefully, will normalize the roads you've been on before, or the one you have now chosen to take with your current partner.

You will be delighted and shocked and, at times, puzzled by the things we do to each other in the name of love. You will be both offended and excited, unable to look away. You may see yourself and those who have passed through your own life, exposing you to the trials and tribulations of simply existing in this world. Somewhere within these psychic wounds of life, for some winning and for others losing, all will eventually find their rightful way.

Both hilarious and heartbreaking, human nature is offered up as fly-on-the-wall observations, allowing for reflection and perhaps some resolve. These stories are yours to enjoy and savor. Indelibly passionate, sometimes dark, but scrumptiously appealing to our primal senses. If you happen to see yourself in these echoes of love and life, hopefully, this book's accountings of mortal narratives and layers of humanity will inspire you to create full and genuine relationships.

It is only human to want to be honestly seen, acknowledged, and adored by the one who captures our hearts.

Dr. Arlene Krieger

Ring the bells that still can ring.
Forget your perfect offering.
There is a crack in everything.
That's how the light gets in.

—Leonard Cohen

1

A MOMENT IN TIME

When you believe in something, stand up for it,
even if everyone is sitting.

—*Natasha Friend*

Dared by her friends to sign on to one of the numerous online dating sites, Charlotte created a basic profile that was mostly the truth with some quirky twists meant to test a man's morals. If a man couldn't answer yes to Sheryl Crow's famous question from the song "Are you strong enough to be my man?" then she wasn't having any of it. By this time in the game, Charlotte was jaded from the disingenuous dating pool—each new encounter stranger than the one before.

She agreed to meet Peter via one of their numerous texts to one another. They had agreed on a local hamburger place that had just opened across from the college.

It was one of those new places that had long lines when it first opened a few weeks earlier.

It seemed that every time she drove by, there were hundreds of people waiting outside. It always struck her as so humanly mundane—the way in which the masses would strategically mobilize, awaiting a hamburger, a movie, just about anything that was brand new. She thought of them as sheep versus independent thinkers. Laughing about this scene whenever encountering it, she would then whisper under her breath, "FOMO."[1]

During their brief initial conversation, Peter had quickly suggested meeting her at the restaurant in an hour. Charlotte didn't know what to make of his spontaneous request, although meeting Peter wasn't her priority, she was hungry. The thought of biting into that juicy burger was number one on her list.

When she arrived at the Burger Shack, she was lucky there were only a few people in line, yet the place was full. Charlotte turned, looking for a man approaching who resembled anything like the guy in the online picture. To her surprise, she quickly recognized him as he walked toward the open entrance where she stood. He wore dark aviators and was thin and handsome with longer hair than had appeared in his pictures. She thought, honestly, he looks exactly like that man from *Easy Rider*— vaguely

---

1 Fear of missing out

remembering that iconic movie from the 70's with the cool-as-heck motorcycle guy.

Peter caught her eye immediately. After winding through the tables and diners to reach her side, he placed his strong hand on her elbow and leaned in to kiss her on the cheek. "Hello, how are you?" he said, grinning from ear to ear. It reminded her of a schoolboy; the sweet innocence to his pearly-white smile. And yet, plainly, this man was experienced in the ways of seduction.

"Do you want something to eat?" she asked, to be polite since she was already at the counter.

"Um, maybe just a milkshake. I ate already."

Charlotte placed the order, and they found a table. While waiting for their food, they sat and exchanged casual conversation. Peter had the kind of eyes that a woman could get lost within. They were blue green, the color of a waterfall cascading into a small emerald-green swimming hole. She remembered a kayaking trip where the guide had advised her that waterfalls which landed in "green water" could be dangerous. There was something different about this man, she thought. "You have great eyes. I like the smile lines, mystical in a way."

He smiled back at her and said, "I like your eyes also."

Their banter was interrupted by the server, and Charlotte launched into her hamburger, not caring what Peter thought of her voracious appetite. *I feel so at ease with this man. I couldn't care less that he is watching me eat like a little kid who has never eaten a hamburger before. I'm sure there is mustard on the corners of my mouth, yet he is still staring and smiling at me with that I've-got-a-crush-on-you look.* Although Charlotte knew this was most likely a "go-nowhere" situation as far as considering Peter a suitable prospect for a relationship, she frankly liked him.

He jumped up to get her straw and napkin as she reached for her lemonade and pushed the plate to the side. This caught her attention and impressed her as most of her dates, who were older men, wouldn't have bothered. It was a simple act, but it meant something to her. They had agreed to a short meet-and-greet as Charlotte was on her way to visit her sister across town. She pulled her keys from her purse, reached for her sunglasses, and shifted toward the end of the booth seat. Peter realized this was her cue to end the date. Grasping the edge of the cold metal retro-diner tabletop, he quickly rose, and followed her lead.

Outside the restaurant, Peter walked her to her car. As she slid into the driver's seat, he leaned in and flirtatiously said "I'd love to come over and go swimming in your pool sometime." She had mentioned to Peter that she liked to swim laps every day for exercise in her backyard pool. Peter continued, "I like to swim naked and lie by the pool to tan."

She responded, "Really...Naked, huh? Um, well, that's nice. I'll think about it." Also, you'll have to pass the test with my dogs. I have a thing for big dogs, can't help it. A lot of trouble yes, but the most loving creatures on earth. We'll just see how my Great Dane and American Bull dog like you." Laughing, he gave her a quick goodbye kiss on the cheek. "Dogs love me, just you wait and see, they'll be putty in my hands once they get a whiff of me."

Driving home, she wondered if she was getting herself involved in some madness. Her cell phone pinged and, aware of the hazards of texting and driving, still she glanced at her phone and was excited to see that it was Peter.

The Texts

Peter: Is your backyard private?

Charlotte: Yes, an eight-foot fence all the way around. Why?

Peter: Perfect, I'm yours...anytime.

Charlotte: Are you sure you don't mind hanging with a woman that's older than you? You could be in trouble, baby.

Peter: If you can handle me tanning naked next to your pool...

Charlotte: I can handle your smart ass (smiling).

Peter: Yes, you can handle my ass all you want. I'll come swim in your pool right now.

Charlotte: Whoa, not so fast. I'm brave, but not that brave. I'd have to warm up to you to have a friend who sunbathes naked in my backyard! You know that old song *"Fooled around and Fell in Love"*—I'm a total fool for love. Don't think

| | I could play sex buddies and not care for you, you know— fall for you. |
| Peter: | I want to be able to tan and walk naked in your backyard. I take my relationships seriously. We might be friends for a long time. |

Weeks later, while out shopping for summer patio furniture, Charlotte heard a text come in. It was from Peter. It was the weekend, and he was asking again if he could come over and swim in her pool. She had not obliged his earlier requests, thinking that if she stayed away from him, she would stay away from trouble. Peter was the kind of fantasy that women dream of but don't necessarily welcome into the reality of their actual lives.

This time, however, Charlotte needed help getting the furniture she had bought from her car onto her back patio. On a daring whim, she invited him over for a swim under the conditions that he would help her put the furniture together and keep his hands to himself when it came to her. He answered, "Absolutely, I will be a perfect gentleman. You know, for the most part, I'm just kidding with you. But I do want to swim and sunbathe naked."

She was confident that Peter would abide by her wishes to be a good friend and nothing more. *Seriously, what's the big deal? If he is willing to strip naked in front of me, admittedly, it's a bit cuckoo, but I'm not going to swoon and faint. I've seen a man's penis before!*

Peter showed up like clockwork.

He helped her lift the heavy boxes from her car trunk into the house and onto the back patio, all the while grinning at her through that award-winning smile of his. Once everything was set up, Peter picked up his towel, sunglasses, and baby oil from the dining room table and headed back out to the pool. Carefully placing his belongings on one of the new chairs, he proceeded to apply baby oil to his upper body, then dropped his jeans and self-confidently Strutted towards the pool.

Charlotte was mixing a concoction of her homemade lemonade over the kitchen sink. Looking up she saw Peter diving, mid-flight into the pool. Trying not to look yet unable to look away she thought I'm acting ridiculous. I want to see him. Hearing her own voice in her head again, *He is so gorgeous, but I feel like a voyeur.* Laughing at herself, she averted her eyes.

Walking out to the pool, she took a seat under the new beach umbrella. Between sipping on the cold lemonade, she asked, "How is the pool water?" Peter was lying face down on the pool float. His body was tanned and well defined. Though thin, he was in great shape and his muscles glistened in the sunlight. From what she saw earlier through the kitchen window; the man was well endowed, and she couldn't help but think of this as they exchanged casual conversation. Her thoughts wandered; *How embarrassed I am…What the hell, I am a grown woman, and yet I feel like a sixteen-year-old right now. Admittedly, I must be losing my mind letting this man swim naked in my backyard.*

Peter was respectful of her wishes to be a gentleman. Staying for only an hour, long enough to tan and a quick swim, he reluctantly climbed out of the pool. Charlotte had already retreated from the summer heat and gone back inside. Puttering around with some laundry in need of folding, she couldn't help but look at him again through the glass doors as he dressed. Unable to hold back her laughter, she thought, now this is temptation, not sure I'll get into heaven for this. It was impossible to look away. *I'm sure I must be imagining this man is interested in me. Maybe it's a casual flirtation but he can't be serious. I'm eighteen years older than him.*

As Peter left, he kissed her on the cheek and said, "Thanks for the swim and beautiful sunny day." She was sure that was all there was to the situation—just a guy looking for a friend.

Two days later, she awoke to a text early in the morning. It was Peter asking if he could come by later to swim. "Sure, I'm working until four p.m., but I'll meet you at the house at five." She thought nothing of it since she had mentioned the trade of swimming pool privileges if he watched her dogs while she was away for a week next month.

Turning the corner onto her street, she saw Peter pulling into her driveway. Getting out of their cars, they smiled, and Peter said, "That was kind of cool, the fact that we pulled up at the same time." Opening the front door to the house, she tossed her briefcase over to the kitchen counter and plopped onto the living room sofa. Peter sat next to her. "Holy crap, it is so hot out. They say it was one hundred and four degrees here today!" Exhausted herself, she uttered, "I'm spent also, so terribly hot out and then into the air-conditioned office and back out into the sweltering heat. No wonder I feel like a wilted piece of lettuce. Would you like something to drink?"

"Nope, I'm going to go sunbathe and have a swim."

"OK, well, I'll be out there shortly." She headed to the kitchen and grabbed a bottle of cold water from the fridge. Still dressed in jeans and a camisole top, Charlotte walked out to the pool and took her usual position under the patio umbrella. She was a natural redhead, with locks of flaming color that went along with a spray of freckles that ran from the bridge of her nose across her cheeks to her shoulders. For Charlotte, the shaded spot under the umbrella was not only her respite from the sun, the thick green canvas was also a safe refuge from the lure of Peter's naked body.

The cliché, "we make plans and God laughs" was one of Charlotte's favorites. That afternoon proved it to be correct. The heat of the day was still steaming off the concrete patio deck. Charlotte walked over to the pool's edge at the shallow end and sat down with her feet on the steps. Peter was swimming laps in the pool, proud to show her a true racing turn. He was once a professional swimmer and still in great shape. She watched with admiration as his tanned and lithe body effortlessly cut through the water.

Still firm in her decision to keep this a friendship, she watched him from afar, though admittedly she was attracted to this man. Suddenly Peter swam up next to her and grasping her wrist, he pulled her fully clothed into his arms and the cool water of the pool. Kissing her gently on the mouth, he held her cradled, locked in his embrace, carrying her around the pool as they laughed together. They talked about anything and everything for what seemed like an eternity. Between words and holding her tightly, he would intermittently kiss her on the lips. She was lost in the blur of his hard body against hers, feeling the pounding of her quickened heartbeat. Although determined not to abandon her own word to keep this simply a friendship— flesh to flesh, she could feel her resolve weakening. Charlotte turned towards him, breaking his embrace, and wrapped her legs around his waist. Her arms around his shoulders now and face to face, she was unable to break free from his gaze. They talked until dusk, exiting only when the mosquitoes finally chased them out of the pool.

Showering the pool water out of her hair, Charlotte was lost in thought in the hot soapy suds as she shampooed her doubts away. Had she made a mistake in not fully responding to his touch? — *Oh stop, let's slow this down…I made the right choice.* Hearing her own voice, she stepped out of the shower into her warm robe. Dressing quickly, she grabbed her favorite pair of ripped jeans and a T-shirt. They stuck to her still damp skin as she struggled to get dressed before Peter.

Peter showered in the guest bathroom, slipped back into his dry shorts and headed out into the living room. "Hey, you want to get something to eat?"

Wanting to pace things more slowly, Charlotte answered, "Thank you. That is so sweet of you, but I have an early day tomorrow."

"OK. Well then, I'll give you a call. If you need anything, just let me know."

The time she had spent merely floating in the pool with Peter, being the recipient of his kisses, was the sweetest she could ever remember experiencing with a man.

On Friday evening, Peter came over after work. It was a beautiful night, and they agreed to hang out, maybe going out for dinner or just chilling at her house. Charlotte, feeling like staying in for the evening, asked if they could just make it a pizza and movie night at home. Relaxing in the air-conditioning she clicked the on-demand channel, scrolling through the listings to see if anything interested her. Peter grabbed a beer from the kitchen and sat down next to her.

Early on in their first few weeks of friendship, they had sipped wine and talked about committed relationships versus no-strings-attached. But they had set no rules for whatever *this* was. Thinking it was a good time to bring up a date she had scheduled with another man on the upcoming weekend. She had previously seen Charles a few times. He was older, an international corporate executive that flew into the local airport, heading home a few hours away by car, every other week. Charlotte casually brought up the subject.

She had been honest with Peter about her concerns, and they had agreed to date other people while they were getting to know each other. She explained that it was mostly because of their age difference and she thought it was best to keep things light between them. Peter listened to her with no response. Charlotte broke the silence, "I swear I can almost hear the Orchid plants breathing its so damn quiet in here!"

After a long hesitation he said, "I guess it's OK. I don't want to interrupt your progress."

Charlotte sarcastically inquired, "You mean my ability to meet a man my age and find a real relationship? Is that what you mean by 'hinder my progress'?"

Peter chuckled, looking straight ahead and not facing her. It was evident that their time together was becoming exponentially more intimate and the sexual tension between them more burdensome. Without responding to her question, Peter abruptly stood up, grabbed his wallet and stared out the window. Turning and heading for the front door, he uttered, "See you later. I've got to go." Perhaps she didn't want to acknowledge his unrest and quick exit and preferred to passively wonder at his aloof behavior. He seemed upset but Charlotte made it a rule to never chase after a man. If he needed time to think things over then so be it.

There was no way that she wanted to go on that date with Charles. She thought, *I know it seems crazy, but I feel like I'm being unfaithful to Peter. What am I thinking? We aren't even*

lovers yet. I hope Peter is OK with this. She remembered how he had mentioned when they first met that he took his relationships seriously—*Am I in a relationship with Peter?*

Later that evening, she texted Charles to cancel their date. She told him she had made other plans as she hadn't heard from him that week. She knew it was a lousy excuse, but she didn't care. Thinking of Peter and wanting to see him again, she texted him to let him know she had cancelled the date with Charles. He sent her back a text saying, "You made the right choice."

Waking up with immediate thoughts of Peter the next morning, she texted him, advising him of storms later in the afternoon and inviting him over for an early swim before the bad weather rolled in. He replied, "Thanks—maybe later. I'm going on a bike ride and I'll text you this afternoon." Charlotte was already anxious about seeing him again. Wondering if he was going to hang out with her in public, not just in her swimming pool, she texted, "What do you think about grabbing something to eat or catching a movie?" She was beginning to have her doubts about whether or not he was purposely keeping their friendship under the radar— mostly because they seemed to never leave the privacy of her home when together.

He answered, "Let's leave that for this coming weekend. I have to jump in the shower...I'm running late to meet a friend."

Feeling let down from their conversation, she tried to distract herself by sitting down at her computer to answer her daily e-mails. Seeing many notifications from the dating site where they had met, she opened the page to look at her e-mail. To her great dismay, there she saw Peter's profile open at the top of the page with "ONLINE NOW" flashing. *Wow, I'm so sick of that stupid dating site.* Of all the things a woman doesn't want to see, it is the man she is involved with, currently online and communicating with other women.

It wasn't so much the fact that he was looking at other women that upset her, after all, she was online herself—it was because he had so quickly terminated their texting and then seemed to have time to jump back online to the dating site. It wasn't even that she felt he owed her anything at this point in their friendship since she was aware that it hadn't indeed morphed into a relationship at all. No, it was more the feeling of dishonesty creeping in. A few untruths that when strung together, seemed to paint an insurmountable white lie.

She was savvy enough—a mature woman still young enough to get into trouble but old enough to know better. She had learned long ago that the mere notion of labeling something, anything, as a relationship after only a few weeks hanging out together was a quick recipe for disaster.

They had agreed to be honest with each other. Peter had previously told her, "Once we become lovers, I won't be OK with you dating other men." She remembered cringing at his possessive attempt to label them as some couple. He made it sound as if once they had sex, she would become his possession.

Charlotte would need a lot more than one roll in the hay to feel committed and swallowed up whole by a lover—not because he had taken her to bed, but because she needed to feel something more than just lust for the man.

She couldn't help but think, *What on earth is going on here? Wow, just another man with DDD—Dating Deficit Disorder! Didn't he tell me that he took his relationships seriously? He's blowing me off, telling me he had to shower, and now he's online talking to other women.*

To describe Charlotte as angry wouldn't even come close to the level of frustration and disappointment she was feeling. She had put her heart out there, believed his words with everything she had in her, and tried to convince herself that the social stigma of an older woman dating a younger man didn't matter. She thought, indubitably, there must have been relationships like this before that had defied the odds. Charlotte thought it best to end the friendship. She texted Peter and told him that although they had agreed to go slowly, deciding to be friends, allowing whatever happened next to happen, she couldn't do this any longer. She didn't understand why he was distancing himself from her and contacting her only at his convenience. He replied to her text, telling her he understood.

The next week went by without much thought of Peter until one early afternoon she received a text.

Peter: "Hey beautiful, it's a sunny day out…I want to cum swim and sunbathe."

At first, she ignored the text, then feeling the need to respond, she replied that she was busy. It wasn't that the sexual innuendo had insulted her. Charlotte was far too knowledgeable in the ways of life—she'd been there done that—even to give it a second thought.

Peter: "OK, I understand. I don't want to invade your privacy."

Charlotte: "Oh come on over. You'll be doing me a favor. I have a contractor coming over who has been nasty to me. It would be good to have a man around the house."

Peter: "Can I swim naked?"

Charlotte: "I don't care how you swim. Just get over here, so I don't have to deal with this contractor guy alone."

Within minutes Peter showed up at the door. The contractor was already there. Peter said hello as he passed through the house, heading out onto the patio with his towel and baby oil. He texted Charlotte from outside, asking, "Can I get in the pool naked? You don't mind?"

"Yes, you can swim naked, I don't care. Maybe the shady contractor will have a heart attack if he looks out into the backyard!" Charlotte looked out through the living room glass doors; standing there talking to the contractor she couldn't help but let out a small gasp as Peter winked at her, dropped his jeans freely and jumped into the water.

Charlotte had aggravated her rotator cuff doing laps in the pool over the last month. After the building contractor left, she went out back to join Peter. Sitting by the water's edge, she kept him company for a short while until the afternoon sun along with the pulsating pain in her shoulder made her weak from the oppressive heat. "I'm going inside to chill out in the air-conditioning and maybe smoke a little four twenty. A friend gave it to me. He said it would help my shoulder pain." Peter excitedly sprang from the water, grabbed his towel, and followed her inside, grinning and as excited as a twelve-year-old schoolboy gazing upon his first dirt bike.

Though they had never been any more intimate with one another than kissing, the chemistry between them was palpable. Strangely, though both were unquestionably experienced in life and love neither had yet made the first move on each other. Heading into the living room, they settled down onto the oversized sofa, nestled in the pillow cushions. Peter, wrapped in his towel, was only partially dry after his swim.

"Don't you go dripping that pool water all over my good furniture and carpet now. I swear I divorced my first husband for sweating on the bedroom floor after his morning jogs," she said, laughing, as she pulled her hair back and began to tie it into a long braid away from the nape of her neck. She was starting to feel a bit clammy. *Is it hotter in here than before?* She thought.

Charlotte felt unusually comfortable with this half-naked man sitting just inches away from her. It was as though they had done this a thousand times before. As he lit the joint, he looked so sexy and manly the way he inhaled just the right amount of the pungent heavenly bud and then exhaled the billowy cloud from the corner of his perfect mouth. Handing it over to Charlotte, she took it gently from his hand and asked, "Are you an experienced smoker?"

"Yes," he said, smiling and trying not to cough as he broke into full-bellied laughter.

Leaning in to kiss her, he pressed up against her as his towel fell aside. They breathed each other in. There was no holding back now. Wrapped in each other's arms, they suddenly pulled apart with a gasp. Charlotte reached for the zipper on her jeans, removing them in one swift motion and dropping them to the floor. Peter's eyes were fixed on her white naked skin, while the deep green of her bikini panties stood out against her flesh. He moved toward her, abruptly pulling her to her feet. Then standing with his hands around her shoulders, he moved them slowly to the small of her back as he lay her softly down on the Persian rug and positioned himself over her. He kissed her once again, this time with purposeful passion—his long wavy hair brushing against her body. Charlotte submitted to his feverish desire.

When they had consummated their lust, both fell back among the scattered sofa cushions in an exhausted fog. Holding hands, they talked for an hour about everything, anything. The evening closed in on them as the sun faded from behind the half-drawn window shades.

Both knew that sleeping together had now changed the friendship forever. Peter said, "Now, don't go changing your mind and getting all upset about this tomorrow."

"What? I don't think I can change my mind at this point. I'm not going to be upset about what just happened between us. We are good—trust me."

Suddenly realizing that he was still sprawled out naked on the sofa, Peter stood up reaching for his jeans. He stepped into them quickly, then ran his fingers through his damp tousled hair and kissed her goodbye. Charlotte walked him to the door, where they stood for a moment, catching each other's eyes in a deep gaze. Those watery pools of deep green—she melted each time she looked into his eyes. Peter smiled with a sheepish grin, casually saying, "Now don't go missing me when I'm gone."

"What are you talking about?" Charlotte asked, suddenly annoyed at his vague statement.

Peter awkwardly replied, "Well, if I'm not around tomorrow or this weekend, I don't want you to get all upset."

"Look Peter, I'm trying to finish a project for work. I have to fly out of town on business next week. I'm just fine. Don't worry about it."

Charlotte gave it her best shot at trying to appear unscathed by his egotistical disclaimer. She thought, *There he goes again, the protective distancing. Why on earth would he need even to make that remark?* He gave her an obligatory kiss goodbye, glancing back toward her as she shut the door behind him.

Charlotte was the kind of woman who was never without male attention. Her beauty attracted men no less ardently than the pied piper and his charismatic flute. But she felt no less of a rejection than any other woman would from the slight of this man's attention. *No matter,* she thought, as there was much to do. The work piled high on her desk needed attention as well as the men in her life. Although a string of suitors pursued her, she felt like Goldilocks and the three bears—some were too small in mind, others too soft in character, most too big in ego.

Peter texted her a few times over the weekend, informing her that he had stayed in and not gone out drinking with friends. She thought the texts were vague yet perhaps they were his way of reconnecting while simultaneously keeping a safe distance.

Grabbing her jacket that rainy evening, she headed out the door into the sticky heat of the summer night to meet her date. This man was gray around the temples—well-weathered in life and matters of the heart. What most appealed to her was that he wasn't looking to put any distance between them.

Charlotte thought of Peter as she realized the struggle of maneuvering through deep emotional waters. She was neither mad at Peter nor attempting to replace him quickly—she knew he would always be in her life in some capacity, whether as a friend or lover. She wasn't sure if it had been him or the social norms that had created the abyss between them. She remembered again the warning the kayaking guide had given to her on that rafting trip last summer: "Beware of green water...it can be dangerous." Charlotte believed in their friendship against all the odds. It did not matter what society had deemed appropriate for relationships between older women and younger men. Some things could not be defined or caged. Though intangible, the heart has a mind of its own where love lives on in time, forever.

2

DESPERATELY SEEKING SUSAN

Love is a second name of sacrifice; once you start
giving, it doesn't hesitate to take...It leaves you
when you are completely vanished.

—Unknown

John and Susan Silverberg had initially come to Dr. Green for marital therapy. They had met online in their late twenties and had become friends over the phone months before ever actually meeting. It sounded like a great story to tell their grandchildren one day. But their story wasn't the picture-perfect fairy tale they had hoped for once they were married.

During that first therapy session three years earlier, John poured out his heart to Susan—his feelings of being on his own with the pressures from work, and Pamela's inability to acknowledge his emotional and sexual needs. John was the youngest CEO to have ever been selected to oversee the southern district's opening of new stores for one of the largest supermarket chains in the country. Susan, trained as a lawyer, was now a stay-at-home mom.

In the beginning, when they were first dating, Susan would show up at John's house and the evening would begin with Susan on her knees, pleasuring John beyond his wildest fantasies. This provocative behavior was not the case for the marriage today. Sex between the two was scarce, and the erotic beginnings now seemed only a figment of John's imagination. There was the addition of three children, the expenses of a new home, and the demands of the young CEO's professional life—all contending for the couple's time and attention. After three years of therapy, the couple showed up each week for their scheduled noon session, continuing to fight over their emotional needs. Each session seemed to be a tug-of-war over whose concerns mattered most.

Dr. Green was an experienced psychologist with over twenty years in the field. Although she had worked with the couple in attempting to understand each other's perspective, sometimes, as they say, "You can lead a horse to water, but you can't make it drink."

Their typical dialogue in session went as follows:

John: "I've had a super tough day at the office. Let me use the bathroom, and I'll be right down to join you with the kids."

Susan: "What? No. I haven't had a chance to use the restroom either—I've been with the kids all afternoon. I'll go first, and you can wait until I come back downstairs."

John: "I've been working all day, and I want to use the bathroom in my own home, damn it."

Susan: "You are such a selfish man. The only conversations you ever want to have are always about you. You come home and try to tell me your problems about work, and it is upsetting my karma. I don't want to hear about your job and fights with your employees. You bring that entire anger home with you, and this is my home, and I want to keep it peaceful."

John: "You are my wife, and a wife is supposed to be there for her husband. Who am I meant to talk to about my day if not for you?"

Dr. Green often wondered where the initial sweetness in their relationship had gone. For a couple to meet and begin to date, there must have been a hook at the beginning, some foundational sameness that led them to believe that they liked each other, had things in common, wanted to date and believed in the possibility of a future together.

Somewhere along the way they had undoubtedly felt they were in love with each other. They had planned a wedding and decided to marry and grow old together—to share a life of birthdays, births, joys, sorrows, careers, accomplishments, failures, homes, travels, family—all this imagined and encompassed in the sixty or so years they had ahead of them.

During therapy sessions, Susan firmly stated that she was no longer the woman whom John had met and married. Her reasoning was skewed in every way possible. None of her thought processes built on the original hook of the relationship; the fact they had once respected, adored, lusted for, and desired to be with one another.

Susan described the role she thought she was now expected to play in this marriage. There were things in her past, in her younger years, that she wanted to erase—too many bad relationships with men, drug experimentation, and issues with her self-esteem. Having met John, a young professional on his way up the corporate ladder, she had decided to marry him and create their new life together.

Both John and Susan, of their own volition, entered their marriage with high hopes of a loving and bright future together. No one dragged them screaming to the altar. Everything seemed to be in place—shared goals, religion, friends, career, status, and chemistry—on the face of it, a recipe for the perfect marriage.

Their therapy continued over a long course of almost five years. Dr. Green was neither in the habit of seeing patients for such a long time nor was it in line with her therapeutic modality. This couple, however, couldn't get it right. Their constant battles over the small stuff, egotistical fights, feelings of insecurity, and aggressive attacks on each other's core values chipped away at the foundation of the marriage week after week.

One of her professors during graduate school had taught Dr. Green that a therapist should never work harder than the couple in the therapy session. The problem here was that the couple wasn't working at all on their marriage. Neither was willing to concede to the other's needs. Susan only saw it from her point of view and didn't care to consider John's stress at work or that he was responsible for hundreds of employees. She accused him of talking down to her as though she was one of his employees. She hated the tone of voice he would use when frustrated. Both resorted to name-calling. Once a couple goes down that route, it is impossible to resume a civil and loving relationship.

Sex between the two had become tenuous at best. John wanted more sex then Susan. Susan showed no interest at all in any mention of the word "sex." She either complained of being too tired or else she criticized John, unyielding in her cruelty, for the way he talked to her in bed, performed sexually, or even for the subjects he wished to discuss outside the bedroom. If he tried to be flirtatious, she would say, "That doesn't sound natural. You seem like a guy in a porn movie." Whatever John said or did, he couldn't win. These absences of tenderness, the limitations, the lack of interest, and the distance from what they once had as lovers tormented him to the point of utter depression.

Not only had the sexual part of their relationship died, but the intimacy between them had dwindled as well. If John attempted to hold Susan's hand at their daughter's piano concert, Susan would pull away and say, "Not here!" She felt that she had a role to play as a mother now and his attempts at any public display of affection caused her discomfort and annoyance. "Susan, I want you to truly think about this, take a minute or two, "Can you describe this role in which you find yourself? It seems to me this is a self-inflicted boundary that you have made up in your mind. We are living in a modern world now. Since when is it wrong for a wife and husband to exchange gestures of love and intimacy, such as holding hands in public?" "I have" she answered defensively. "He is so *touchy feely;* I can hardly stand it. Why must I show him affection in public, we hardly touch when we're together in private—unless of course he is trying to give me a back rub and then you realize of course Dr. Green, all he wants from that is sex."

In the end, the therapist advised the couple that if they weren't willing to compromise and acknowledge each other's feelings, needs, and desires, then the relationship was doomed.

The dynamics between the Silverberg's appeared to feed off the turmoil they created in their lives.

Each was so eager to win, to make sure that their "right" was their partner's "wrong." How could this marriage have a chance if there was no middle ground, no safe place for the couple to come together out of love and respect for each other?

Dr. Green ended their sessions, as she felt they weren't willing to do the work that it took to have a successful marriage. Making that call to John wasn't an easy thing to do. Advising him that she needed both partners to "*actually work on the marriage*" and until that was happening, she had to terminate their visits. "Take some time to think things over; I will be willing to re-open your case file for you and your wife; however, all games must cease on Susan's part and she needs to decide if she truly wants to save this marriage."

Dr. Green had always implemented and demanded the four critical elements of a stable and prosperous relationship in her work with patients. These consisted of respect, dedication, commitment, and trust. Along with these four central tenets of the relationship, she also insisted that the couple bring forth character traits of compassion, generosity, forgiveness, and intimacy; character traits necessary in order to examine and re-create healthy relationships that would survive. It was almost impossible to believe—this couple exhibited none of those qualities in their marriage.

Dr. Green had assumed an ethical vow to help and heal. Often, she would bring her work home with her and be unable to sleep, her patients' issues going around and around in her head. She cared about her patients but had to walk a fine line ethically between being their doctor, not their best friend. Unfortunately, as the adage goes … "How many therapists does it take to change a lightbulb? One, but the lightbulb has to want to change."

3

CAPPUCCINO WITH A
SLICE OF BDSM

Youth ages, immaturity is outgrown, ignorance
can be educated, and drunkenness sobered, but
stupid lasts forever.

—Aristophanes

JJ often flirted with Carmen when they saw each other at the gym. In his mid-fifties and in good shape, JJ seemed harmless enough, although the sexual undercurrent in their conversation was clear to those that cared to notice. They exchanged phone numbers and kept in touch randomly through text messages. JJ had always been the initiator in their conversations, asking her things like, "Are you married yet?"

Every few weeks she would get a text message with the same sarcastic blurbs. He traveled for business often, and several months passed before she heard from him again.

She was surprised to see a text come in from him early one morning. JJ, on his way out of town again, asked her if she would be open to meeting him for a drink upon his return in a week. She replied, "Sure, but you do realize that I don't know anything about you, except for your name, and the fact that you go to the same gym where I work out."

He answered, "We have chatted for months now. What else do you need to know? Let's meet and find out more about each other."

The following week, on a rainy Wednesday evening, Carmen met JJ at her favorite café. Not knowing whether this was a dinner date, she had eaten before going out to meet him at seven. It was hot and muggy, so they went inside. While deciding where to sit, he asked her, "Coffee or something to drink?" *Thank goodness I ate before I met him here*, thought Carmen, *because this is totally a cup-of-coffee date.* Approaching the counter to order, she asked the waitress for a cappuccino and a blueberry scone. JJ asked for water.

At this early moment in the date, Carmen already figured she was in for a rocky evening. If this is how it's starting out, with a man who ordered only water, she wondered, *Oh boy…what else am I in store for tonight?* She knew that JJ drove a new BMW and was semiretired. It wasn't as if the man couldn't afford a meal with a top of the line luxury car parked outside. So then why would someone order water, she wondered, if he planned on enjoying the evening and taking some time in getting to know her?

Already uncomfortable, she randomly chose a table next to the window and exit door. Perhaps subconsciously she wanted this to be over sooner rather than later. They sat and exchanged information about careers, life, love, and family. At first, she was impressed with this man. He had spent a lifetime in service to the country in the armed forces as an army major. His descriptions of risk, challenge, and voluntarily going back for further tours of duty were truly admirable. If you asked Carmen's friends, they would tell you she was always hoping to meet a man's man. She wanted a man she could finally trust. Staring into his eyes she asked herself, *is this the kind of person whose shoulder I can imagine resting my head on?*

Approximately one hour into the conversation, JJ brought up the subject of sexuality and stories he'd written that he often posted on Facebook. He bragged he had a "fan club" of women who followed him—boastfully admitting that he liked to rile the women and reveled in their reactions to his provocative short parables. The subject of different scenarios was brought up, and then he said *it*—the *it* of all questions that set Carmen into an internal rage. "So, are you into the BDS and M? I'd sure like to get my hands on you someday." He chortled with a wicked grin. She just stared at him, thinking, *I'm sure he thinks he has me enthralled at this moment, ugh! BDS and M—he can't even pronounce it correctly!*

"Ha, you want to see something amusing?" As he pulled his cell phone out of his pocket, he scanned through until he came to a photo. Leaning into her across the table, he proudly showed her a picture of himself and his ex-girlfriend in bondage outfits. "I'll tell you about this some other time," he said with a sinister hiss. His snickering laugh sent chills up her spine.

JJ's lame attempt at seduction only repulsed her. It settled in her stomach like a lead weight, as she felt a wave of nausea come over her. Trying to control her dislike for this poser, she asked, "Whatever gives you the idea that I'm interested in this conversation? I hardly know you."

He answered her with a wry smile, exclaiming, "Because I know that once you trust me, you will enjoy it." Knowing that trust comes with time and respect for another human being, she tried to contain her laughter. Carmen had experienced this behavior before with men on first dates. Little did these people know she had them all figured out way before their impotent attempts to captivate her with bondage lingo, and way before they could guzzle down their lattes, or choke on the first bites of sashimi. If you listen carefully, a man will tell you who he is in the first twenty minutes of conversation, no matter what the day, time, or scene. She was armed and ready for JJ's insolent proposition—good thing he wasn't eating on this date.

Though she was neither a close-minded nor biased woman regarding varied sexual proclivities, appetites, and lifestyles, she now felt on guard and disrespected by JJ's weak attempts at being alluring. She was a lawyer who had raised two young daughters on her own, working her way through school, often working two jobs at a time. She had seen and heard almost everything on her long journey as a single woman over the years, and it was this life experience that brought her to be the woman she was today, sharp as a tack and nobody's fool.

This line of conversation from JJ was, in her opinion, nothing more than an immature taunting, an attempt to get a reaction from her. He knew nothing of the real Dominant/Submissive relationship, or he would never have approached the subject in such a synthetic way. Only a novice, a phony, someone who was attempting to attract her into a belief or entice her into the supposed sexual activities he believed to be BDSM, would have approached the subject in such a manner.

Carmen was proud that she had worked her way to success and had never depended on dating or marrying a wealthy man to help her survive. She was not a taker or a user and after her divorce she had never lived with a man or played a man for money. A self-made woman, Carmen was much more substantial and worldly than she appeared to be from first impressions. She liked to refer to herself as "simply complicated"—a woman of many faces and facets, more comfortable in jeans and a T-shirt, not likely to drop two grand on a purse or a pair of shoes. Often people tried to get over on her, as they mistook her kindness for ignorance. Her life had taken her down many roads. She knew who she was and what she wanted in life: a lover and a partner. Yet only a man who had veracity could ever hope to get her attention.

During their friendship there had never been any implication that she was into any alternative lifestyles. JJ had failed to see her for the woman she was; a woman that would never settle for being insulted on a first date. She had felt insulted not just because of JJ's suggestion of the "D/s"[2] relationship and his ignorance on the subject, but even more by his total disrespect and inferences of sexuality over a cup of coffee. Who was this man to assume that he could speak to her of such things? Because they were friends at the gym? She thought, *This man has no boundaries...and no filter on his mouth or his brain.*

Carmen said, "You know, I've mentioned some of my nightmare dates in casual conversations with you at the gym, and I know that one of those versions I told you about was about how men are so crazy in this city, either wanting to hook up right away or play bondage games. And now you are sitting here and daring to tell me that one day, once I date you and trust you, I will want you to tie me up? And the fact that you say, 'I will have you' is a total turnoff for me."

JJ's only comeback was, "Oh come on, you know I'm just trying to push your buttons—maybe not every night, but at least occasionally I'd like to tie you up—you're going to love it."

Maybe wasting her breath on this man wasn't worth it, but she continued. "Whatever happened to a man taking a woman out on a date and getting to know her? You know...the old-fashioned way? I believe it's called *courting*," she said with conviction. "I think sexuality that grows out of intimacy is an amazing kind of sexual connection. Did

---

2 Dominant/Submissive

you ever consider that approach to being with a woman?" What bothered her most about the evening with JJ was his complete ignorance about the lifestyle.

Carmen was aware at this point in the conversation that he had it all wrong. A real D/s relationship is a very particular and specialized lifestyle. In many ways, the lifestyle is a beautiful commitment to one another. It was an agreement to adhere to the boundaries set. It is not about "cuff them, tie them up bondage activities," and she well knew that was where most men and women have it all wrong.

Carmen knew with the advent of the movie *Fifty Shades of Grey*, the hype of handcuffs and leather whips propagated the idea that the supposed illicit activities of a "BDSM"[3] relationship—not the norm of the customary regular "Vanilla"[4] relationship could bring a new sense of sexuality and intimacy.

Men most often seemed to have a discombobulated idea that their prospective dates or lovers would find it sexy. Her friends typically found the subject matter or dating come-on a clichéd turnoff. Some called it "mommy porn," referring to those who were bored or exhausted from the humdrum of motherhood and marriage, and

---

3 BDSM: bondage, discipline (or domination), sadism, and masochism (as a type of sexual practice).
4 Vanilla: sex with no kinks

who thought that bondage games would add a thrill to their relationship.

Carmen was well versed in the D/S relationship. She hadn't made known to JJ that she had once been in a relationship of this sort with a wonderful man a few years earlier. Nor did she bother to inform him of the real beauty and intimacy she experienced in the lifestyle within the ritualistic and supportive respect and honesty of such a contractual relationship. Explaining these dynamics to this lothario was like putting lipstick on a pig. He was only interested in the titillation of his perception of BDSM, never caring to explore the lifestyle in its entirety.

Carmen laughed, thinking of the *New Trend* in fashion called "athleisure" or "activewear," where clothing designed for working out or for yoga was changing the way women dressed so that there was spandex in everything! Shopping for a pair of jeans that didn't make her look like she was dressed for a night out on South Beach was impossible. Her brow was furrowed in deep thought as she asked herself, *Is this bondage foolishness now a new "Dating Trend?"*

JJ interrupted with a loud and insincere, "So what's up baby, care to get together this weekend? There's a ZZ Top tribute band playing at Giblin's Irish pub this weekend."

Reaching for her purse, Carmen ignored his invite. "It's getting late, and I have an early morning start. It was amusing meeting you, though I don't think we'll be seeing each other again.

He replied, "Oh yes, we will, and at some point, you'll like to be spanked. Listen, baby, I am a retired army major currently a deputy U.S. Marshall, Special Services Division. I'm not one of your local namby-pamby police officers or firemen. I'm going to do things to you that no other man has ever done. When I'm through with you, you'll throw rocks at other men. I want you to ride me like I'm stolen."

She laughed thinking of a T-shirt she saw a few weeks ago at the local Walmart; gauche and loud, the pink iridescent letters shouting against the black cotton had read, "Bored Before It Even Began."

"No, you listen. I have already gone out on three previous dates with men over the past few years. Two were claiming to have been FBI or CIA secret agent men, and one claimed to be a professional sniper. "Is that all you've got?" she asked mockingly as she leaned over to grab her belongings from the back of her seat.

Moving her chair away from the table, she slung her purse over her shoulder and abruptly stood up. JJ quickly came over to help move the chair from behind her, giving his best try at a gentlemanly effort. *Really, at this point, he's going to be respectful. A botched attempt at best to be genuine.* Though wanting to exit the date as quickly as possible, she wasn't angry—just resolved to accept the man for who he was and not interested in getting to know him. She had learned that to vilify a man would only turn the anger inward and result in frustration and negative thoughts. Forgiveness is a hard lesson to learn—how to give it and release that energy back into the universe. Each of us is on his or her own course in life. Our unique paths and the choices we make as people were not Carmen's to judge that night.

Walking her to her car in the rain, he reached out and placed his hand on the small of her back, guiding her safely around the large puddles of water. He took her hand several times but released it each time he moved his hand back to her waist, leading her around the parking lot until they reached the car.

Carmen turned to him to say goodbye. He reached up and smoothed away a wisp of hair from her eyes, fondling the golden strand for a moment and then laying it against her temple, as though pondering his next move. Then quickly leaning in, he kissed her on the cheek before he turned and walked away without saying goodbye. She watched him walk to his car. He never looked back. It seemed to her that he had gotten her message loud and clear. She took no prisoners, and the major knew it.

Though abrupt, it was a fitting end to the evening. Carmen tossed her hair over her shoulder as she slid into the car, buckled her seatbelt, and drove off, heading for home.

She had lived her life so far with unstoppable hunger and determination to stand on her own two feet. She was unyielding in demanding respect and a fully integrated purpose from any man. Carmen, as the saying goes, "was a force to be reckoned with," and most men recognized that. If not, they didn't have a chance with her from the start. Her friends often told her, years into their friendships, that she was the most optimistic person they had ever known, even when confronted with many of the seemingly insurmountable hurdles in her life.

No one was going to destroy Carmen's light and joy of life. She knew in her heart that her self-essence was hers alone, to decide to keep or give away. There would never be doubt in her mind as to who she was, and what she would and wouldn't accept from a man, especially this type of man.

Turning up the radio, the corners of her lips curled up into a smile as she drove off into the night. She thought, the right guy is somewhere around the corner. I'll wait for him to show up, and we'll share a slice.

4

THE GURU AND THE PORN STAR

Life is like sex: if you want a happy ending,
don't rush.

—*Paulo Coelho*

Jennifer's birthday was just around the corner. She knew this should be a particularly great day, but she was reticent to admit to herself she would probably be alone. Her best friend was out of town, and she had broken up with her boyfriend just a few weeks ago.

Approaching the weekend, the sound of her voice kept rattling around in her head. *Seriously, I'm a big girl and will be just fine doing something for myself on my birthday. I have earned the right in life to enjoy the day doing whatever I want to do that pleases me!* Sitting alone in a local restaurant that she often visited for lunch, she was surprised when the man at the next booth leaned over towards her and asked if he could join her.

They were the only two people in the restaurant aside from the girl on her cell phone. "Well, um, I suppose so… I'm just here for a quick lunch and I'll be leaving shortly." The girl at the table behind her was incessantly talking on her cell phone. It was one of the habits of people in public that Jennifer abhorred. She thought that a conversation with this man who had such a friendly smile and kind eyes would calm her and mute out the girl's loud conversation.

His name was Spencer. That struck her as a funny thing, a sign, as that name was one that Jennifer had dismissed as a choice for her son's middle name. She believed in karma and symbols from the universe. Spencer advised the server that he would be sitting with Jennifer. He picked up his cocktail, slid into the booth facing her, and dropped his keys and mirrored glasses on the tabletop.

Noticing the sunglasses, she cracked a joke about having a pair of those glasses herself, commenting that they were her favorite glasses and he was just a copycat. It was her attempt to break the ice and start a conversation. Spencer seemed oblivious to her wit. But as he began to talk, she noticed that he had a northeastern dry sense of humor. Spencer launched into a long tirade of his transcendent quest, his training with gurus, and the philosophy that he was following—filling in the cracks with his long background, as a retired management executive from the New York City area and his divorce of six years ago.

The man was well dressed, an expensive watch on his wrist that implied success, which corroborated his claim of being semiretired from his job of thirty years in high-level corporate business. He was self-educated and proud of that fact; trained by the school of hard knocks and had only a partial college degree. Finely pitched in the ways of the world from the rigors of Wall Street, he bragged about his home up north, his ex-wife, their two daughters, declaring they were still good friends after the divorce. He didn't stop at that. He also relayed that she had been an overbearing mother and he thought she had done a dis-service to their daughters by smothering them.

Spencer had a different spin on parenting and went on to describe why he wasn't encouraging his seven-teen- and nineteen-year-old daughters to attend college. His thoughts on higher education were clear. He didn't believe in getting a college degree. In today's world, he proclaimed, a college education would take one only so far and he insisted his theory on real-life street smarts and experiential knowledge was the only way to further one's career and life. He boasted of climbing the corporate lad-der on his own, achieving his high-level executive status. Nevertheless, Spencer was bitter and disillusioned at the end of his career, supposedly sabotaged by his colleagues through deceit and deception, ultimately resulting in a buyout and his early retirement.

Jennifer honestly gave him her best effort at full atten-tion, but his discourse seemed to go around winding curves into otherworldly places, the stuff of secret societ-ies. Somewhat confused, she didn't dare delve any further into the subject matter for fear of insulting him.

Switching to the subject of where he was from, Jennifer questioned him about a journey he had taken around the world. Anything to get away from this didactic lecture of spirituality. Jennifer was herself interested in the studies of mysticism, anything esoteric and metaphysical, but she was turned off by anyone that would force their belief systems, whether devout or heavenly, down someone else's throat.

She offered up a brief background of herself, as he hadn't asked her too much about her life. Giving him a quick synopsis of her training as a young surgeon, and her early marriage and untimely divorce, she paused to see his response. After all, this man had just informed her that when he met his sacred maker (a guru type who had inducted him into his respected secular orbit) he entered a state of being which he had no control over.

Suddenly, Spencer said, "I was speaking in a different tongue with this man, as though I was channeling the information…It never happened again since that day in New York twenty-five years ago, but it changed my life forever." Jennifer thought, most certainly, this man will have something prolific to say about my journey in life.

Spencer stared at her through those brown eyes, pupils flecked with gold, reminding her of that magnificent yet lethal panther that wounded the young girl recently at the local zoo. *What kind of fool tries to take a selfie against the cage of a beast so powerful?*

"I think we have a lot in common with regards to a *"spiritual path"* I'd love to tell you about my life- changing experiences. They started about 25 years ago when I had fallen very ill…" Before she could finish her sentence, Spencer blurted out, "Umm, OK, can we talk about me for a bit?" That was the red flag that Jennifer somehow either missed or chose to ignore. His statement felt like a quick blow to the face, cold and abrupt. Perhaps she had just let it be at that moment, too stunned to acknowledge his rudeness. He'd shown no interest in her personal story, only a cold and selfish rejoinder demanding the focus of the conversation return to him. Uncertain as to the character or actions of this man, she refused to believe that there wasn't something more profound underneath—some worthwhile layers perhaps unexplored. Always looking for the good in people, she found that her optimism in life was often also her weakness.

Jennifer had to get back to work, and Spencer had driven in from out of town on business. As the skies threatened with dark clouds and clapping thunder, both said goodbye and ran to their cars before the drenching rains began. They had exchanged phone numbers, and Spencer had promised to call. Though he wasn't exactly her type, his intellect interested her, and she thought perhaps she would give him a chance in getting to know him if he bothered to call her.

It had been a busy week at the hospital. Jennifer had stopped at the grocery store after work and was carrying her groceries in when she heard her cell phone ringing. It was Spencer. She picked it up, telling him that she'd get back to him shortly once she had made something to eat.

He said he understood and hadn't eaten either and told her he'd give her a call back later in the evening.

Spencer called her back as he said he would. In retrospect, when Jennifer looked back on the beginnings of their relationship, she repeatedly questioned why she had even considered getting to know this man. The writing on the wall was deeply rooted in her mind, something to be realized sooner rather than later. Why she had set out on this endeavor would haunt her for weeks afterward. In the end, Jennifer knew better, but like a moth to the flame, she flew towards Spencer's charismatic and obscure nature.

He had invited her out for her birthday, asking her to choose any place that she would like to go to that she hadn't frequented before. "How about Paris?" she laughed as she offered up the suggestion.

"Not until we are sleeping together," he replied. Laughing off his off-color remark, and unfortunately used to these snide comments among the dating pool, she had become immune to the offense.

"Well then if you insist…I just love the Waldorf Astoria resort. I've been there before, and I'd love to go again."

"OK, then the Waldorf it is. I'll make the reservations." Spencer's verbal gestures of grandeur were intended to impress yet they fell flat on Jennifer's ears once he alluded to her "sleeping" with him. She may not have been a woman of the world, but she was mature enough now at the age of thirty-nine to know when words hit her the wrong way.

She thought, *I'm almost forty and the pickings are slim as of late. Are there no sophisticated men out there that know how to treat a lady?* Not sure of what to make of him, she let his rude and crude remark slide, just chalking it up to machismo males in their late-40's. She laughed out loud, thinking, *Why must men on the other side of getting old— act like they've never had sex before.?* She knew there was no Mr. Perfect out there, and most of the men she had met were either threatened by her career, trying to take her down a notch or two, or were simply buffoons.

Pulling up to the valet, she stepped out of the car where Spencer was waiting for her. Holding a single red rose, he handed it to her and leaned in for a kiss on the mouth. She turned her head slightly so that his kiss would land on her cheek. He seemed to ignore this awkward moment, took her by the arm, and led her up the walkway into the hotel, and down the opulent hallways to the entrance of the restaurant.

Spencer pointed out his expensive off-white dinner jacket and told her how he was proud of his newly acquired Italian-made couture clothing. Jennifer thought he looked like a throwback to Gatsby's time, and not in a good way. Spencer carefully seated her at the table and then sat down across from her. Quiet and contemplative, he began to speak in measured tones and questioned Jennifer about her way of relating to the world, asking her whether she engaged people from her head or her heart. She answered his questions one after the other until it appeared she was taking an oral exam in college. Realizing that she was now not only uncomfortable but also put in a position of defending her views, she blatantly told him her feelings.

She also thought this was the proper time to make sure that Spencer's bumbled attempt at romancing her over dinner that night didn't also include an expectation for her to accompany him to his hotel room. He had told her earlier that he had taken a room to access the private restaurant and this way he wouldn't have to make the hour's drive back home later in the evening. Pushing her plate away and taking a deep breath, she blurted out, "You know, I'm not going to your room after dinner."

Spencer abruptly dropped his fork to the plate and shouted, "You have just ruined the evening! How can you even say such a thing—to even think that I would expect you to go to my room?" His manner was now cold and accusatory. Jennifer was seething inside, as the man's excuse of booking a room and checking in so as not to have to drive an hour back home was just ridiculous. He had already hinted over the last week that he intended to have his way with her—and the sooner, the better. His nasty attitude now only served to close her heart to him completely.

Flustered and irate at this point, she said, "Who are you to define how I think and relate to people or the world? How dare you tell me I was coming from my head and not from my heart? Your disparagement of education and its purpose in our world is an underhanded comment. No... definitely more like an attempt to undermine the rigors of my academic career—when you say I have accomplished much, but the education means nothing."

He replied, "I used to know a porn star when I worked in the media field in New York. She and I dated for a while. She was a true healer in working with her clients."

"You mean she was a prostitute and a porn star?"

He replied by saying, "No...she was a healer and had clients who paid her for her services. What makes you think that just because you're a doctor, patients want to come to see you? Doctors kill people all the time! Maybe there are people out there who would prefer to see the porn star and partake of her healing powers versus traditional medicine."

At first, Jennifer thought he was kidding her. But no, there on his face was the conceited stoic look of one that professes to be all-knowing. She said, "Did you just compare my entire education and career as a doctor to a porn star?"

"Why, no, I'm not comparing you. I'm just saying there are people who would prefer to find someone in some nontraditional, healer modality, you know, like my porn star friend rather than someone in the conventional medical field." In one fell swoop, this man had achieved the impossible—completely erasing Jennifer and her life's work off the board. Somehow, she just felt sorry for him that he saw fit to dress her down verbally and reduce her professional achievements to the same level and expertise as a porn star.

Too caught up in this demeaning attack, she had spent most of her birthday dinner defending the education system and explaining why licensed professionals spend the time to educate themselves. She had been through many years in academia, believing that she could provide a service to people—a professional service with guidelines and mandates to not cause harm.

Standing up from the table, she watched in slow motion as the white linen napkin dropped from her lap and fell across the plate of mostly untouched, cold food. She hurriedly thanked him for dinner and headed for the exit. He rose suddenly with clumsy verbal attempts to stop her, begging her to stay. She turned slightly, looked over her shoulder and shouted, "No! For a guru of the ages, you are an insensitive and egotistical fool and nothing more than that. I have always heard that if a man is truly enlightened…he will never proclaim to have reached 'enlightenment.'

> *There are two kinds of light—the glow that illuminates, and the glare that obscures.*
>
> *—James Thurber*

5

SUGAR DADDY GONE WRONG

Since when did we become the voice of reason?
Sooner or later you play all the parts.

—Unknown Author

They were a beautiful couple. Clyde's British accent made him even more handsome. Louisa was much younger with an exotic Latina flair. Clyde and Louisa had come to therapy seeking help, as their marriage was out of control. "Hello, I'm Dr. Selma Champion, welcome to my office. Please be seated and make yourselves comfortable," she said warmly. During this initial session the couple disclosed bits and pieces of their sorted stories, and their interpretations of aggressive behaviors towards one another; ultimately divulging the reasons for why they were currently involved in a torrid court battle.

The police along with the court system, attorneys, restraining orders, and veiled threats against each other were now ongoing and egregious. Their daily actions were both conspicuously wrong and offensive, including Louisa's claims of fear for her life having him thrown out of their ten-million-dollar home and put in jail, based on her accusations of Clyde's behaviors, both numerous and despicable. "He beat me and threatened, I'm going to have a van pull up to the house, and have you taken away where they will never find your scattered body parts." Now they sat before the psychologist looking to see if there was anything left to save of the marriage.

The transgressions in the marriage were numerous, and both parties were blameworthy in their infidelity. This disloyalty might have been expected from Clyde; he had a long history of womanizing ways. Louisa, however, was a novice, a woman-child with dreams and expectations of a luxurious life—yet certainly not pure in her intentions.

An individual session was scheduled for Louisa for the next week and then the doctor would see both Louisa and Clyde for their weekly alternating individual sessions.

Clyde dropped Louisa off for her session as he had possession of the car keys for both their vehicles. Louisa's attempt to crash into Clyde's Rolls Royce several weeks ago had reportedly left him doubting her sanity.

Louisa was elegantly dressed in a simple black sheath dress with black stilettos sporting a small mink pom pom at the back of each heel. She appeared downhearted and reported feeling discouraged from their first session. "I thought he would be more understanding and respectful of my feelings. I know things have gotten a little crazy, but

I know he wanted us to live in an *'open marriage'* he said so himself."

Perched on the edge of the office sofa, Louisa leaned in and whispered softly, "He is not an angel you know, while I was gone, he was living with a woman his age along with her two children, while I was gone this summer. She eagerly gave an account of going back to her country for some plastic surgery. While there, Louisa had also taken a lover and boldly divulged this to the doctor expressing no shame.

Dr. Champion asked curiously, "Why did you get plastic surgery? Was there a physical problem? You are so young, what did you have done?" Louisa responded, "Oh, I went for pussy rejuvenation...Do you want me to show you? I had lost weight, and my pussy was hanging too low." She stood up, motioning to her pubic area. The doctor vehemently replied, "No, no...that is OK. You don't have to show me. I understand what you had done."

Leaving after her session with the doctor that afternoon, Louisa paused. Leaning against the door, she looked the doctor up and down and said, "I can see why Clyde comes to you. He likes 'grannie ladieeess'...You are his type."

The doctor was confused and asked, "I'm sorry. What did you say?"

Louisa repeated, "grannie ladieeess'...you know, the older women. He likes that. You are his type. That woman he was living with while I was away in Colombia was in her forties, ugh...older!"

Dr. Champion looked at Louisa in disbelief, taken aback by what she had just heard. Speechless she thought to herself, *I've got my work cut out for me with this one. Of course, she has no respect for her twenty-five years-senior new husband. This girl respects no one, not even her doctor. She stands proudly in her expensive new clothes and newfound lifestyle, yet her crassness shows through like a dingy light, casting its harsh yellow brashness on her store-bought prestige.* Sadly, as fate would have it, no matter what you dressed her up in, Louisa's greed and shallow interior would color her future.

They came to therapy for several sessions. Clyde had paid up front for ten sessions. The doctor was never sure if he had invested in treatment for the 10 percent discount or because he had a sincere interest in investing in the therapeutic process, thus hopefully saving his marriage. He had been married several times over the years, and from the details Louisa revealed of his philandering, the man could easily have given Don Juan some severe competition. Handsome, wealthy, and with the charm of a movie star, Clyde seemed indisputably intent on not having another failed marriage.

Hoping that things were going better for the couple, the doctor was surprised to see them back just two days later. This time they had called and asked to come in separately. Neither knew of the other's appointment that day. Clyde had been removed from the home by the police after a phone call from Louisa and a subsequent restraining order that had been granted to her by the courts. The purported charges were that he had attempted to harm her, threatened her, and held a knife to her throat during an argument the evening before.

Now all bets were off as far as the couple resolving their marital conflicts. The respective attorneys were involved, and the young wife was out for blood. She poured her heart out to the doctor, telling her of her lover in Colombia and plans for them to make a life together. Louisa felt that she was owed money and lots of it, and she had plans to fight the original marital agreement to the death.

Clyde had tears in his eyes for a moment while describing his disappointment with his choice of marrying a "shop girl." "She was nothing when I met her, just a girl who could hardly speak English and was overweight...we were just friends in the beginning." His sadness was not insincere as he regretted failing at yet another marriage.

The doctor requested to see them again, together as a couple, hoping to find a hook, a foundation in the marriage, a mere semblance of love, respect, or dedication which could have been enough to save the marriage. They showed up in separate cars and entered the office. To Dr. Champion's surprise they exhibited civility toward each other. This new behavior might have been a good sign if not for the treacherous and menacing tête-à-tête that was to unfold in the next hour. Between Louisa's threats of having Clyde killed by the Colombian cartel and Clyde's promise to have her deported immediately, you might say things didn't go well in therapy that day. Trying to neutralize the situation at hand, the doctor now asked despairingly if they would be willing to come in over the next two weeks for separate sessions.

Clyde had been living out of the house waiting for the scheduled court date regarding the outcome of the restraining order Louisa had placed on him. Louisa was living there alone for the most part, other than a girlfriend staying over occasionally. Clyde had been ordered by the court to stay out of the house during the two-month probation time frame and mediation. His attorney had done an excellent job and was able to prove that this was not the couple's first dance within the court system.

They had been separated earlier in their eighteen-month marriage, and Louisa had already been far-reaching in her requests for money, a change in the marital contract, demands for vehicles and Clyde's commercial building investments. The judge had denied the monetary changes and claims, rescinded the restraining order, and allowed Clyde back into the home. One might wonder what the judge was thinking—allowing these two people back under the same roof? This couple's life so far had been a catastrophe just waiting to happen. Indeed, within days, all hell broke loose again.

The police were called out to the home by Louisa early on a stormy Monday morning. Clyde was in the process of moving back home but hadn't even packed his things from the penthouse suite at the W Hotel—his home away from home over the past few months.

Before the ink could dry on the judge's orders for Clyde's return, Louisa was claiming that Clyde had broken into the home the previous evening and had stolen her $98,000 Patek Philippe watch. Crying hysterically, she claimed her husband had given her the watch as a wedding gift. Mustering up a deceptive calm, she whimpered, "He is trying to destroy me. Don't you see his games?"

Clyde was advised of the situation and taken to the home by way of his attorney. When they arrived, the police were there trying to defuse the situation while Louisa was in a state of hysterics, screaming and eventually throwing a glass vase at Clyde. This time, however, Louisa was removed from the home by the police. The officers were aware of the lifting of the restraining order, and from their vantage point, along with the judge's reports, this woman had cried wolf one too many times. It was all too apparent this was a last-ditch effort to vilify her soon-to-be ex-husband.

Clyde had also reached his breaking point. In his heart, he felt betrayed by this girl—a young woman who had primarily come from nothing and was now living the high life he had provided to her. That hadn't seemed to mean much to Louisa. She challenged him on every platform possible: his earnings, investments, business decisions, and moral compass. This young bride seemed to have no boundaries when it came to greed and her sense of entitlement, nor did she have any fundamental understanding of what their marriage would entail and the short part she would play in it.

There was no good guy or bad guy here...both were the villains, partners in crime, in the demise of their marriage. Though both were at fault in their failed union, neither should have been surprised at the outcome. Louisa knew way before she agreed to marry this man that he was a wealthy playboy with several past marriages. Clyde's history of relationships and his lifestyle were clear. What was there to question about the history of his numerous unsuccessful prior marriages and indiscretions—the cards were on the table before she nose-dived into this disaster.

Louisa would have forgiven him one indiscretion, but he had been sleeping with other women during the entirety of their short marriage. Although she had agreed to a *'swingers' lifestyle'* the adage of "what's good for the goose is good for the gander"[5] didn't appear to thwart her jealousy of Clyde's trysts.

Louisa was equally accountable in this twisted road of collusion and marital bliss. She had once provided Clyde with one of her girlfriends, having asked her to come fuck her husband as she hid in the closet and watched. She supposed that this would excite him, turn him on—keep him more interested in her as she invented the role of his free-spirited young wife.

Clyde knew that his double-dealing ways wouldn't change, and yet he expected his new bride to accept whatever transpired between him and other women. It seemed to the doctor that her patient had led his young wife to

---

5 used to say that one person or situation should be treated the same way that another person or situation is treated.

the seductive feast and was then dazed and distraught when she ate from the hands of the devil. Perhaps this fledgling bride was persuaded by Clyde's desirable and exciting lifestyle—his romantic and deceptive approach. Was she equally to blame for the crimes of their marriage? Unquestionably yes. As to her unspoken agenda for this marriage; guilty as charged.

As the saying goes, "best-laid plans of mice and men oft go astray." The marriage ended. Louisa went back to Colombia with the expensive clothing, shoes, and jewelry she had accumulated during the union and the agreed-upon terms of the original prenuptial agreement, barely enough money to survive a year and certainly not in the lifestyle that she had become accustomed to while married to her wealthy older husband. As for Clyde, he retrieved the scattered ruins of his machismo and ego, safeguarded his fortune, and quickly moved on to another young thing that he had met along the way.

The doctor saw him one last time. He had swung by to say hello and let her know that everything had worked out OK. His quandary of whether to salvage this marriage had been settled now to his satisfaction, and somewhere in this quagmire between hell and heaven, he felt redeemed in the outcome.

Dr. Champion attempted to warn him of selecting young women who might be swayed by his affluent life-style, trying to insinuate themselves into his life and, unfortunately, bringing locusts of destruction into his wealthy and pleasure-seeking ways. No commitments or responsibilities, no ties that bind—this seemed to be the life to which Clyde was most devoted.

The doctor was reminded of the story of the scorpion and the frog—a tale touting that some things never change. A frog is a frog, and a scorpion is a scorpion, doing what a scorpion does best— bringing the demise of both the scorpion and the trusting frog. Giving her a quick hug goodbye, the doctor accepted his embrace and said, "You are always welcome here, and you still have paid sessions available, please use them." She never saw him again. Over the years, when thoughts of past patients came to mind, Dr. Champion often imagined that Clyde had found happiness at last…somewhere, somehow.

6

THE TIT-FOR-TAT MARRIAGE

*I was seldom able to see an opportunity until it
had ceased to be one.*

—*Mark Twain*

Simon and Pamela Bach were both professionals in their late thirties. They had agreed to see a therapist, as their marriage had numerous problems. They had decided to see Dr. Sexton as the therapist of choice. At first glance, Simon was a good-looking man with a pleasant demeanor, impeccably dressed. Pamela was tall and rail thin with curly-blond hair, not as beautiful as her husband was handsome. A mismatch of sorts; it seemed to work for them at first glance. Dressed in frumpy garb, aside from her four-hundred-dollar espadrilles, she appeared to be confident, yet her brazen front was merely a mask for her insecurities and anger, which had boiled up inside her over the years.

During the session, Simon was outwardly confident that they could resolve their issues. Although Pamela said the right words—blah blah blah, "Yes, I'm here to see if we can fix this marriage," it was clear within minutes that she was going to use this session as an outlet to stake her claim on the misery he had caused her over the years. Her mission seemed clear; rip his balls off, leaving the poor man both emasculated and embarrassed. With whatever speck of masculinity he had left, cringing at the far end of the sofa, all that Simon was able to muster in retort to her verbal attack was a futile attempt to defend his position.

Pamela worked while Simon attended law school. Having helped to support them back then, she now felt that he owed her a lifestyle in which she wouldn't have to work. Pamela thought she had paid her dues and had a right to enjoy some of the fruits of her labor. Since Simon had become a successful attorney, she wanted to retire full time and stay home with the kids. Pamela had continued to pursue a professional career and achieved earnings of a six-figure income while working as a realtor. Simon was not crazy about her giving up her job, as their combined salaries helped to pay for their lifestyle and ongoing expenses.

Simon was worried. This was nothing new as Simon was troubled about everything most of the time; the economy, taxes, the new home expenses, their lifestyle and credit card bills, and the fact that no one's business was doing exceptionally well in this economy, not even corporate lawyers.

The couple's taste and way of life were not simple—a million-dollar home, private schools for their three children, memberships to the local club, and traveling with friends to the local hot spots during the season. Simon had recently moved them to this new home from a smaller and cozier neighborhood, as he thought it a good investment and wanted to be on the water.

Their marriage on the outside looking in seemed a perfect life. They had it all—the home, lifestyle, and perfect kids. It wouldn't have been so bad if Pamela was a genuine partner and had given a damn about her husband's feelings or concerns. Instead, she was bitter and resentful, often brutally demeaning him behind his back with criticisms of not only his manhood but his physical appearance as well.

Though Pamela abhorred him, Simon was successful in his career and well respected among his friends and peers. So, it was with great oddity that Pamela hated this man with a jealous vengeance. She hated him even more for having a life of his own, finding that male friends enjoyed hanging out with him and other women found him attractive. Once, while Pamela was out of town, Simon had gone out on his boat with friends from work, including several single women. Finding out about the boat outing upon her return home, she was livid that one of the single women had contacted Simon, asking him to hang out that weekend. Though they were old friends, Pamela wasn't open to sharing him. It was now evident that though she didn't want him, no one else was to have Simon either under Pamela's watchful eye. Pamela played dirty and dressed this man down verbally to the core of his existence. She betrayed his privacy in every way imaginable, exposing chronicles of his supposed awful childhood, plastic surgeries, and adolescent issues. There was to be no end to the total disparagement of her husband—from his professional abilities to his performance in the bedroom. She irreverently told Dr. Sexton, "Simon is an unattractive man and a coward. I can't stand him. He isn't even a good lawyer. No one likes him at his firm." Irreverent in every way imaginable, this woman truly despised the man she had married. No matter which way the therapist attempted to help the couple work through the issues within their marriage, the 'Bachs' relationship was inherently doomed to suffer a dreadful fate, an inescapable destiny. Pamela wasn't interested in divorce. She vehemently said, "If I have to suffer, he has to suffer." She had aimlessly given some thought to going back to her home state and leaving the children with Simon. It seemed at times that she just wanted to be done with "*this thing*" as she called it; the marriage that she found herself helplessly lost in.

Pamela was anywhere and everywhere with her wild plans of escaping the marriage, and yet she remained solid in her conviction to never divorce.

Whether it was out of fear of losing the lifestyle, for the sake of the children, or merely to save face with their friends, Pamela was unyielding in her decision to remain married to Simon. In the session, she said, "I can't stand him. I could do without the sex also."

"I don't understand. Why on earth then would you want to stay in this marriage?" asked Dr. Sexton.

Pamela apathetically replied, "Like I already told you…I don't want to be divorced. No one in my family has ever divorced before—it would be embarrassing."

At the next session, the couple argued about who got to do what in their free time away from the children. Simon wanted to go fishing with his friends. Pamela resented his "boating time" and preferred to windsurf on the beach.

The arguments were relentless in who deserved what, and which of their desires took precedence over the other's allotted recreational time. Interestingly, none of their arguments ever included them doing things together, sharing in some downtime that would bind the two in cohesive and enjoyable activities. You know the old saying, "those that play together, stay together."

Life had become unfathomable. Simon couldn't even supervise or discipline his children without Pamela's attempts at discrediting him in front of the children. If Simon said his daughter should drink more milk, his wife argued with him in front of their seven-year-old daughter, saying that their daughter drank enough milk during the day, so as not to have to drink milk at breakfast. Pamela's purposeful attacks and resulting deterioration of Simon's role in parenting was beginning to create a severe problem for everyone involved, especially the couple.

Pamela divulged to Dr. Sexton in a private session her side to a recent conflict with her husband. She told her their child had recently overheard a phone conversation between Pamela and Simon about where the family was going to eat that Friday night. Simon wanted to leave work and meet at a pizza restaurant close to home. Pamela didn't want pizza and wished to order takeout. The couple quarreled for a few minutes, and Pamela reluctantly agreed to meet him at the pizza place. Their daughter, sitting in the kitchen and listening to her mother on the phone, looked up from her video game and asked, "Why do you listen to him? Can't we go back to our old house and live there without Dad?"

The destabilization and deterioration of this marriage was confirmed by Simon's questions to the doctor during his next solo session. Simon was noticeably upset. There was no mistaking his anger and disillusionment with the marriage. Now he was asking the therapist, his words tumbling from his lips in a confused and hasty manner, "I think I may want to get a divorce. Do you know of any good divorce lawyers in the area? We have been married over fifteen years now, and I think they are looking to change the divorce laws soon, perhaps allowing the wife lifetime alimony if the marriage is over sixteen years. Our anniversary is next week, and that will make our marriage a total of sixteen years."

Although the marriage was on very shaky ground, Dr. Sexton wasn't in the business of leading her patients toward divorce. There had only been two couples she had worked with in her twenty-five years of practice that seemed to warrant no other options other than divorce. Yes, the marriage was in deep trouble; however, Dr. Sexton didn't believe in making any rash decisions when a relationship was in crisis. She felt that if it took many years to get to such a ruinous liaison, and the couple should at least attempt to make a solid and committed effort to save it.

Simon went on to say that there was a history of mental illness in his wife's family and that he was worried about the possibility that Pamela may have bipolar disorder. He thought she should see a psychiatrist he knew of and that she should most likely begin treatment along with medications. He had high hopes that this might save the marriage.

Dr. Sexton didn't think it could hurt, although she was against medication unless first properly diagnosed and prudently prescribed by a psychiatrist. It was a surprise at first that Pamela agreed so readily. This woman's agenda, however, was plain to see at her next session. She made it clear that she had decided to see the psychiatrist in hopes of getting her husband to feel sorry for her. With this plan in place, she had every intention of going on with her openly aggressive behavior in the marriage. Pamela said, "This way if he thinks I am nuts…then I can get away with whatever I want and blame it on my depression."

Although Pamela had agreed to it, Dr. Sexton had been worried that Pamela wouldn't keep her appointment with the psychiatrist since her husband had insisted on it. To Dr. Sexton's dismay, Pamela had gone to see the referred doctor and created a plan precisely to her liking. The next week she walked into session with Dr. Sexton managing a wicked smile—she was the cat that had swallowed the mouse. Holding a book in folded arms close to her chest, she confidently said, "the psychiatrist I saw last week gave this to me. This is going to be a mind-blowing solution to all of my problems."

Pamela took pleasure in the psychiatrist's disclosure—though to Dr. Sexton this seemed impossible, and perhaps simply a fabricated tale. Pamela basked in her own gluttonous joy, stating that the psychiatrist knew her husband through the local church, and from what he knew of him he could understand why she was having such problems with Simon. Dr. Sexton would never know the absolute truth of what had transpired that late afternoon at the psychiatrist's office. She had not personally referred Pamela and therefore wasn't privy to the doctor's notes. It seemed both unprofessional and unethical that a psychiatrist would have uttered such a blasphemous statement about Simon, primarily because he was a medical professional, and Pamela, his new patient, exhibited labile behaviors—a hot mess at best. No licensed mental health professional would ever have gone down that road.

At five-hundred dollars an hour, according to Pamela, the psychiatrist had just assuaged her concerns and relieved her of all responsibility for the part she played in the crumbling marriage. Still clinging to the book, he had given her to read, Pamela insisted that all would be fine now. She thought that she merely needed to acknowledge how difficult a man her husband was and find a way to live with it. After all, in her mind, she was not guilty of any wrongdoing in the marriage. Apparently, in Pamela's world, it was the man—this man that she was married to who was causing all the problems.

Dr. Sexton placed a call to Simon that afternoon. She informed him that she was no longer willing or able to work with them as a couple. She advised him that if his wife was pointing the accusatory finger at him and unwilling to work on the marriage collectively as a couple, she would not be able to help them. She said, "I'm sorry to say, but I don't believe your marriage has a good chance of success. If you should both decide to come back and be fully responsible for the respective roles you play in your relationship, and can be fully engaged in therapy with full honesty and respect for one another, then and only then, will I be able to see you as patients in my office. I hope you will make the choice to continue with therapy."

The seasons changed as the year passed. The couple never came back to therapy. Scooping soup into a bowl one winter afternoon at Whole Foods, Dr. Sexton looked up to see Pamela standing next to her. She was placing boxes from the salad bar into her cart. Startled, she burst out, "Oh hello, Doctor, I saw the article in the New York Times that you wrote this past fall about couples and marriage. I showed it to Simon, but I didn't tell him who had written it. You know how he feels about you." Dr. Sexton smiled knowingly at Pamela, thinking, *OK, if that's what you need to tell yourself—funny how I, the therapist, am now the villain in their marriage.*

She felt that one of the most disappointing things about being a therapist was to want so very badly for a marriage to work itself out yet be unable to help these people move forward with their relationship. She knew when couples rejected therapy and turned the other cheek to their hopelessness and pain—in a desperate attempt to maintain the homeostasis in their home—they would often pretend that nothing was amiss, no matter who suffered. Dr. Sexton grew a thicker skin each year into her private practice, knowing that the separation of personal feelings and professional care could ultimately leave a professional therapist with no way to assist the couples.

Her main lesson was something she needed to remind herself of daily: If one person in the relationship has an agenda, and is unwilling to acknowledge, compromise, or have empathy and compassion for their mate's point of view, it is almost impossible to help the couple save their marriage.

Unless, of course, they stay due to the finances. In this couple's story, that is exactly what transpired. To split their assets would have left them in a financial lifestyle that neither would have wanted.

Only when people have taken more abuse than they would give to themselves do they eventually face the dire straits of their relationship—the misery and dreadful future they are to endure together. Hopefully, at this point, the victimized person in the relationship makes that brave decision to move on, no matter what the cost. One can only change him- or herself. True and lifelong partners need the human qualities of compassion, empathy, and dedication to the relationship.

Pamela was both vapid and self-absorbed, lacking in human compassion—living in her self-created bubble and pointing fingers, selfishly defining the parameters of the relationship. One-sided partnerships can't exist. Without a cohesive flow, there is no possibility of a couple ever surviving a marriage.

Dr. Sexton gave them her best efforts in therapy, and as the saying goes, "Don't shoot the messenger." In love and light—to those who wander blindly.

7

THE ART OF GUT INSTINCT

*Don't compromise yourself. You are all
you've got.*

—Janis Joplin

It was a hot summer day, and Arianna, anxious for the weekend to come, jumped into her jeep and headed to the hair salon to get a whole new look. She had trudged through magazine after magazine looking for a haircut that she could live with during the hot and humid summer. *Why be mediocre?* She thought. *I'm going for the whole shebang!* She knew that her choice of an original shorter style would keep the long, thick, honey-colored mane of hair off her neck and it would be easy to manage in the ocean. Her Instagram handle was "surfergurl," proudly boasting abundant selfies of her addiction to the sport. At thirty-six she found she was pretty good at it and fell right into the hang of her "takeoffs" along with other surfers' half her age. She loved the idea of a new look and was choosing to go blonder, sort of a tough girl, biker look, but more feminine—the kind of blond that melts men's hearts.

Arianna was a fair surfer, but it was also about her fashionista self. She loved the "Abyss" wetsuits almost as much as the waves. The new haircut would match her new sexy silver one perfectly! She could be a bit narcissistic about her appearance, yet she wore her tendency towards vanity with a good splashing of humility and kindness—balancing her ego and drawing many faithful friends her way.

A holiday weekend was ahead. The thought of having four whole days of chilling out, the beach, and hanging with her friends was driving her crazy as she counted down the days to the weekend. With her new blond appearance, she was ready for anything this Fourth of July!

Still single and heading toward the big forty, she had tried the online dating scene for a while, finally deciding against it. The variety of guys whom she had met had either lied, showing up ten to twenty years older than they said they were, or were married or separated. These experiences had turned her against this dating venue. She ran screaming for cover, believing that this was not a way for her to meet a supposedly eligible man.

Arianna's friends were always begging her to come out and head for the hot spots, local clubs in the city, which were about an hour away from the small town she lived in. "No," she replied. "There's just not much out there for me.

Everyone wants to get drunk or get laid, and I'm looking for something real."

Finished with the haircut, she felt free from the heat of the summer, yet she was worried that she had made a mistake. As she stared down at the beautiful strands of her long golden hair being swept away by the hair stylist's assistant, that nagging feeling of doubt crept in. Leaving the icy cold of the mall, she walked out into the rush of the 102-degree smothering summer heat. *Thank goodness, I cut my hair short,* she thought as she walked to her car, keenly aware of the beads of sweat already forming under her cotton tee. The decision to cut her hair confirmed and done, and with a renewed bounce in her step, a reaffirming smile appeared across her face. She thought, *What to do with my day? Which errand shall I do first? I so want to go to the beach!*

Along with her newfound love of surfing, she had been swimming all summer instead of adhering to the monotonous routine of going to the gym and was pleasantly surprised to see the muscles developing in her arms, abdomen, and thighs. Feeling great about herself, both physically and mentally, she headed home to change into a bathing suit, grab a towel and beach umbrella and head out for her swim at the beach. Lean and slightly tanned she unknowingly turned heads when walking through the local beach's snack shack to grab a smoothie. *Ah, the beginning of a beautiful afternoon,* she thought as her feet hit the hot sand.

Arianna had achieved everything she had wanted out of life at this point, having switched from one career to another. She had left law school to go into the field of medicine. She was now a physician's assistant at a local doctor's practice. The only thing missing was that one great guy. Earlier in the week, before she had taken down her online profile, Arianna had agreed to meet Paul for an afternoon iced tea. They had planned to meet later in the day, before the madness of the weekend. Although she had met this man on the dating site and had sworn to herself that she was done with this inane way to meet a good guy, she had agreed to this date at the last minute. *What the hell, one more date, and on a Fourth of July weekend, what can it hurt?* Feeling uneasy about their plans to meet all day and realizing that she truly had a pounding headache coming on, she quickly picked up her phone and texted Paul, canceling the date.

Something he had said in their previous conversations had rubbed her the wrong way, so she didn't feel bad about her decision to cancel. She thought, *After all, I do have a headache, and it looks like rain is headed this way.* It was hard to say just what he had said to cause that icky feeling in the pit of her stomach, yet there it was, and she decided to listen to her impulses. Her head was now throbbing, as dark black storm clouds were rolling in off the sea towards the shore.

Paul immediately returned her text, questioning her reasons for canceling. He was irate and informed her that several women had canceled on him at the last minute over the previous few weeks. Not sure how to respond to this, she hesitated for a moment and then texted back.

Arianna (2:30 p.m.): "I'm sorry…I honestly have a terrible headache. Maybe we can get together over the weekend?"

Paul (3:45 p.m.): "Lol…at the gym. So, you need medical attention? Lol, but I did cancel a neat booze cruise my friend was having at three o'clock…I understand, though. Call when you feel better…real…"

Paul (3:51 p.m.): "Well, I tried to call you…no answer. Hope you're not in the ER!"

She searched her phone for a confirmation message back from him, needing to know that she was off the hook from this dreaded date. There it was. She must have missed his texts while she was grabbing her beach gear and running to the car in the rain. Looking at his messages, she got that funky feeling in her belly again, *Something just doesn't sound right with this guy.*

Paul (4:05 p.m.): "Uh, Paul here. Calling you back. Just got out of the gym—anyway…so you have a headache. Hope you feel better. Yes, I probably sound a little jaded. I am. Nothing personal toward you at all… last-minute headaches, and I'm sure you have one… just sad, I guess…was sort of hoping we could at least meet. Oh well, ibuprofen should work, put ice on it… and try to go to sleep. I hope you feel better. Ok… goodbye."

Texting was not one of Arianna's favorite things. There was the fact that he had told her that she wasn't the first to break a date with him at the last minute. She thought that odd, wondering to herself, why numerous women are breaking dates with this man? *Hmmm—something's got to be off here.* Nevertheless, she called Paul back. The phone rang several times with no answer. She tried him once more and then left him a message. Explaining that she didn't like games and wasn't playing one with him, she apologized for the hasty retreat from meeting him that afternoon.

It was around 9:00 p.m. when Arianna was awakened by the sound of texts coming in. She often slept with her cell phone on her bed in case of an emergency with her elderly mom who lived across town. She had taken a Motrin and gone to bed early that evening, dozing off while watching some late-night television. It was Paul, texting to apologize and begging her to meet him the next evening. He pleaded, "Can we start over?"

Paul was obviously anxious to meet Arianna. He apologized profusely for his accusatory attitude and further justified, again, how he had recently experienced several women who had broken dates with him at the last minute. Knowing that she had done the same at times, often due to her busy work schedule or sheer exhaustion come the weekend, she understood how this could have happened to him. "Well, I'm not one of those women who broke the date because I had something better to do. I basically developed the most splitting headache...sorry for bailing on you, but I wasn't feeling well."

He replied, "It's all good. I want to meet you. I'm going to the gym in the morning, and then I want to meet up with you. How about sometime this July Fourth weekend? I'll drive to you, as we are about thirty-five minutes apart. Please, sweetie, I think we could be really good together."

Again, Arianna got that funny feeling, a sense of doom and that voice in her head, a red blinking light, warning her, "look out ahead." This man seemed a little too gung-ho...remembering his words "really good together," she thought, *That's jumping the gun just a little bit.*

It was the end of the July fourth weekend, and Arianna was driving back home from the beach. Tired from the visit with her friends but still high-spirited and in a festive mood, she wondered where she could see some fireworks later that night. Her phone pinged, and she looked to see who was messaging her. She was surprised as she hadn't heard from Paul for a couple of days. He had left a voicemail. As she listened to his message, his words, eagerly spoken, were sweet and pleasant asking her to meet him for a drink at the local sports bar that night. She struggled with her own thoughts on the ride home. Sometimes the right decision about who to date and why confused Arianna. If she condemned every fault that men had, there would be no one else left on earth to date. Or so it seemed to Arianna that night.

Though she had been firmly resolved to not meet Paul, her overly analytical nature acquiesced. In the aftermath, she attributed her decision to his self-professed honesty, causing her to yield to his pleas of joining him at the local pub.

Feeling carefree in the late-afternoon heat of the last day of the holiday weekend—wanting to believe those good guys do exist out there somewhere, she thought, *Oh whatever, it's just a drink. Maybe I'm wrong about my feelings about this guy.* She returned his call and agreed to meet him around 5:00 p.m. He had asked her to meet at the same local sports bar he had requested days before. Assessing the bar location in her mind, she concluded that there was open access to the parking lot. *I can get out of there quickly if I don't like the guy.* Arianna thought she had it down to a science, as far as knowing how to protect herself out on the street.

As she walked in, Paul approached her immediately, heading up from the back of the bar where he had been sitting. He was much more muscular than he had appeared in his photos. This man looked like the Hulk on steroids. Arianna followed him back to where he was nursing his third beer. She slid onto the bar seat next to him and ordered an iced tea. He immediately ribbed her about not drinking and pushed hard to get her to order a drink with some alcohol in it. She reminded him that they had talked about her not drinking—at all—in their earlier conversations. He just laughed at her insistence that she didn't imbibe alcohol of any sort. Arianna attempted to change the conversation.

The minutes seemed like hours—tick...tick...tick, as Paul's voice droned on about his past marriage, the affair he had with his wife's best friend after the divorce, and more about him. Every few minutes or so, Paul would lean in touching her thigh as he spoke. It was the kind of touch that magazine articles talk about, for dating safely—the light grazing of the hand against the prospective partner to make contact, an ancient primordial instinct used by the opposite sex to show their interest in their mate.

Glancing at her watch, she noted that she'd been sitting there for exactly half an hour. They had agreed over the phone the week before to make it a quick hello, no longer than a half hour. It was Paul who had insisted they stick to that thirty-minute timeline. Arianna was fed up with men who wanted an audience to talk about themselves. Paul hadn't asked any questions about her life as he was too busy talking about himself.

Without a moment's hesitation, she opened her mouth and heard her own words echoing in her ears. "Paul, it was nice meeting you, but nothing is going on here between us. I mean...you know, no attraction for each other." Not wanting to hurt his feelings, she willingly put herself out there and stated, "You're not attracted to me...right?"

Without hesitation, Paul said, "Um, no...I mean, you have nice hands and all."

Arianna took that comment as her chance to escape from the date and said, "OK then, well, it was nice meeting you." Jumping up suddenly from the barstool, she gave him the "air cheek kiss" and said, "Goodbye—take care." Darting straight for the door, she was out of there like lightning. Glancing over her shoulder to make sure she was in the clear, she could see Paul staring down into his beer. He seemed to be in a trance, as though he didn't know what had just hit him.

In a way, Arianna felt that he deserved the quick exit. However, often her worst downfall in the dating process was being too nice. Not wanting to hurt someone's feelings, she felt compelled to give him a call on the way home. Her main intent was to make sure she had left him with a sense of just wanting to be friends, and not that he was Attila the Hun in her eyes—and that she hadn't meant to humiliate him.

Paul was not interested in any friendship. Arianna's quick exit had been a distinguishing moment of no return in his eyes. He resolved to be enemies to the death, to crush any chance of ever being civil to Arianna again. Now a raging inferno, he would make it revoltingly clear that he wasn't going to take too kindly to have been dismissed by a woman.

The Texts

Arianna: "So, do you want the truth?"

Paul: "About what?"

Arianna: "About why I had to restrain myself from wrestling you to the ground and strangling you to death. Why I interrupted your conversations. Why I wanted to hit you over the head with a brick. But I still understand you are just human—a person who is trying to figure out life, your future, like all of us are trying to do.

I am telling you this as part of our friendship. OK? You talked about your ex-wife for twenty minutes and then your ex-mistress who was married to someone else for the next fifteen minutes."

Completely ignoring her efforts to be civil and explain her frustration and quick exit from the date, Paul broke into more aggressive and vengeful retorts. The texts flooded her phone.

Paul: "Great. Mostly I was disappointed with your lack of intellect, continuity, and deceit of personal appearance. Your personality drifts from one character to another...all are dull physically. Never mind, I won't hit you with that. Just not like the brochure. You're ordinary, stupid, lack confidence, and...not attractive. You owe me gas money. What a fucking waste of time, and I tried to be nice. You're an unattractive sick bitch and should be not be helping anyone! A physician's assistant? Yeah right. You're messed up, and you know it. What a hack! You're now blocked...dumb ass. Oh, one hundred and twenty-seven pounds. Pffff, try one hundred and eighty! Lose the lard! OMG...never again! Yuck! Oh...part of our friendship. Fuck off."

Arianna: "I didn't lie to you about anything...Wow...why are you acting so crazy? Why are you being so cruel? I have no hard feelings...I left because

	we both agreed there was no chemistry happening, and we had prearranged on the phone to be honest with each other at first meet-up. To set up a time limit of thirty minutes flat. Seriously, get off the steroids!"
Paul:	"Steroids? You fat outta-shape pig. I bust my saw to stay in shape...no drugs...You make me sick, Again, Fuck off!"
Arianna:	"I'm sorry that you are so angry. I didn't mean to dis you or be mean in getting up and saying goodbye. I've upset you. It wasn't a rejection. We merely met, talked, and honestly didn't have much in common. Anyway, good luck, Paul, and please get some help. Perhaps some anger management wouldn't hurt."

Arianna had decided to exit the texting battle civilly, attempting to defuse Paul's aggressive name-calling, and before riling this madman up any further. Ending the conversation, she realized she was a lucky girl. The fact that she had accidentally pushed Paul's buttons merely by being honest with him had served her well. His aggressive words were signs of his lonely insecurity, desperation to be liked, and his uncontrollable viral hatred when he didn't get his way. "Dear God," she said out loud to herself, "I hope other women are aware of how many odd birds and evil characters there are out there!"

In retrospect, she wondered why she hadn't adhered to her original decision not to meet this guy. Her gut reflexes had indeed kicked in. Her common sense had finally shown up, though almost too late. She pondered the scary logic of it all. *Is this how some women end up missing and murdered?* Inspired by her dangerous liaison with this wretched character, she knew what she had to do now.

There would be no more laissez-faire decisions when her senses told her *No!* If she couldn't qualify the man before meeting him, that would be it. No further meet-ups without vetting the person first, either through social media or one of the online sites that verify people for a fee. She had heard of these treacherous experiences from some of her friends, dates that had been cheap, rude, malicious, even putting one of her girlfriends in a choke hold.

Now having experienced some of the unsystematic insanity within this diabolic dating realm, she finally realized that the perverse flaws and cracks of casual Internet dating just weren't for her. From then on, Arianna created a self-standard for her dating life, a mantra—repeating it over and over in her head, quietly in a meditative calm. She would use this chant whenever she found that she doubted her intuition.

If ever alone on a holiday weekend, I will occupy my alone time with someone I like and admire—Me! I promise never to challenge my sixth sense about anything or anyone again.

The mantra was to become her sacred word for weeks to come until it was drummed into her memory bank forever. Whenever she would be tempted to go against her initial feelings, in a milky mode of meditative consciousness, she forever more would drift back into the recesses of her mind, remembering a fanciful saying—

Be who you are and say what you feel, because those who mind don't matter, and those who matter don't mind.

—*Dr. Seuss*

8

IN THE NAME OF LOVE: THE PREDATOR

Whoever is dissatisfied with himself is continually ready for revenge.

—*Friedrich Nietzsche*

It was after-hours yet despite the interruption of her dinner, Dr. Weatherspoon picked up the cell phone. She knew it was a patient attempting to reach her, as she used this second iPhone to transfer the incoming office calls to personally monitor the phones. In the business of a private psychology practice, it was difficult to differentiate between those patients who were in dire need of speaking to her and those who just blatantly ignored her business hours.

A familiar voice on the other end pleaded for a few moments of her time while rushing into a tirade of duplicitous reasoning for wanting to help his new girlfriend. Finally taking a breath, he identified himself as a patient from eight years ago. Sam was a rising star, a mid-level executive, a career man with a marketing background; arrogant as all get out and damn proud of his smug demeanor. The doctor remembered him. It was impossible to forget his displays of bad temper and screaming fits that he had exhibited in therapy years earlier with the woman he was married to at the time.

Sam and Barbara, his ex-wife, had attended several months of therapy back then, to no avail. Most of the sessions involved him shouting her down and Barbara begging for another child to keep their recent baby company in the coming years, although she admittedly despised her husband.

Thinking this ludicrous idea was the most nonsensical declaration she had ever heard; Dr. Weatherspoon exhausted all therapeutic attempts to reach a place of compromise with the couple. After Barbara, in one of the last sessions, divulged that the most recent explosive fight had involved holding on to their infant daughter, struggling and grasping for control while cursing each other out in their front yard, the doctor asked, "Have you both considered divorcing at this point?"

Sam glared at Dr. Weatherspoon and stated, "I thought we came here for you to fix our marriage, not advise us to get divorced!"

Dr. Weatherspoon never heard from either of them again after that session, at least not for eight years—not until today's desperate pleas from Sam to help with his new relationship. He was both agitated and angry as his words gushed forth to describe the circumstances with his new girlfriend. "She is the most beautiful woman. Gorgeous, like a model," he said proudly. "Her name is Tiffany, and I adore her."

She was thirteen years younger than him, a young mortgage processor, working in the same building as Sam. They had passed each other in the elevator numerous times without having spoken. He wanted her badly and knew from the moment he had laid eyes on her that he must have her. He was aware that she was involved with another man and didn't care. He would make her his no matter the cost.

He relayed the torrid tale to Dr. Weatherspoon, leaving no detail unturned. It was a jumbled mess of who was sleeping with whom at the time, betrayals and underhanded behaviors from all involved and entangled in this web of seduction.

The current situation was tenuous at best. Tiffany had been "Baker Acted" a few weeks earlier by her family, at Sam's prodding. After he had spoken with her sister in upstate New York, Tiffany's family felt it necessary to carry out preventative steps to ensure her safety, as Sam had advised them that she had made a threat to take her own life in a text message to him earlier that month.

The details of the recent dynamics between the two lovers, their brief but sordid history together, the disreputable circumstances of Tiffany's past traumas and other male "friends" and Sam's ex-girlfriend's degenerate stalking were all the makings of a bad soap opera—perhaps even worse, a B-grade horror flick.

Sam's self-professed love for this new woman was heart-wrenching at first glimpse. Had the man finally become human? Could the doctor dare to hope for human sensibilities within this man? It was almost believable, except that Dr. Weatherspoon knew Sam's history well enough to suspect deception somewhere in his narrative. His earlier marriage was disastrous; his arrogance had permeated every marital session like an unsavory odor wafting through the room. Both ego and anger led to the destruction of Sam's earlier marriage. Now, back in therapy again, it was clear that appearances can often lie. It is a well-known fact that those skillful in using well-crafted words may craft and generate many untruths over time.

Dr. Weatherspoon's research over the years had unveiled that the difference between a liar and a person telling the truth is founded in the use of unique variable words in the recounting of a story. However, Sam's accounts of his story never varied. Each time he would describe the abusive relationship, he blamed all on Tiffany—a well-rehearsed litany, each word carefully chosen to denigrate his partner. Judge and jury had spoken in Sam's mind, and Tiffany was to pay the price if she stayed.

Sam had offered to pay for Tiffany's sessions out of his purported concern for the girl. At this stage of the game, he wasn't sure that she would stay with him and not revert to her old behaviors of casually going from one man to the next. However, she was now in his life and his bed and he vehemently demanded that he be given a reduced fee for her twice-a-week visits with Dr. Weatherspoon.

On the day of their appointment, Sam strode in with a ubiquitous attitude; he appeared both oppressive and rude as he strode in ahead of Tiffany. Dr. Weatherspoon felt a lump rise in her throat as she struggled to swallow; her words muffled and stuck in her craw. Dr. Weatherspoon was a tough old bird, raised in the rural South by rednecks, educated rednecks with college degrees and money—being called a *Georgia Cracker* would be considered a compliment to this woman. Not much ruffled her feathers. She barely mustered an utterance of a greeting. "Hello, Sam, it's been quite a while since we've last met." Sordid flashes of him from eight years earlier quickly raced through her mind.

He was a small thin man, well-muscled with a craggy face—far from handsome but charismatic in a Napoleonic-complex sort of way. He had a surprisingly deep voice for such a tiny man and used it often in therapy to overcompensate, she believed, for his insecurities and to attempt to control the situation. Tiffany was tall and lanky, with the palest white skin and long flowing dark hair. She appeared sad and vulnerable, reminding Dr. Weatherspoon of Snow White before she bit into the poison apple.

She suddenly felt goose bumps on her forearms as she stroked the sleeves of her silk shirt to warm herself up. Her eyes followed the girl as she sat down. Tiffany, in jeans and stiletto heels, settled into the safety of the dark leather sofa. Sam plunked down next to her. Leaning forward with his legs spread apart, Sam grasped his hands firmly in front of him, elbows on his thighs, as he stared across the coffee table into Dr. Weatherspoon's eyes.

As they began the session, he spoke of Tiffany and the dynamics of their living together. Rudely maligning her opinions and perspective on their living together and his heavy drinking, his critical words stripped her of any human decency or self-worth. Tiffany sat frozen with her legs crossed in the opposite direction of Sam. Her body sunk into the folds of the soft leather, listless and unremarkable in presence. Her role in this sordid connection was that of a victim. Regrettably, women who become and see themselves as victims usually have no idea who they are, never having become an autonomous human being. Perhaps not of their own fault, but straight talk, still a victim.

In this case, Tiffany's sense of self-worth was nonexistent. It would be kinder to say that she was codependent, just playing into Sam's drama. Yet, that was not the case. Tiffany was dangerously invisible in this relationship. Sometimes those women who completely lose themselves in a relationship, swallowed whole by their man, cease to exist. In this case, Dr. Weatherspoon was essentially hoping to keep her alive, working carefully to extricate her from Sam's slimy grip.

Going along with Sam's request to see his girlfriend for therapy sessions twice a week, Dr. Weatherspoon attempted to break through Tiffany's barriers. Her experiences with earlier men and currently with Sam had left her crippled in fear. Unsure of herself and only a hollow shell of a young woman now, it concerned the doctor that it would be a difficult task to help Tiffany see her way clear of these dire circumstances. This situation wasn't just a verbal-abuse situation, but rather, Tiffany's life was hanging by a thread, both emotionally and physically.

From several of the self-reports she had reluctantly relayed to Dr. Weatherspoon, there had been both mental and physical abuse from Sam.

"Oh, but I love him," she said.

"What exactly is it that you love about this man?" the doctor asked.

"He was there for me when the guy I was sleeping with last threw me out," she said.

Dr. Weatherspoon implored, "And now, please tell me...is there anything else about Sam that can explain why you continue to stay with him when you say you often fear for your safety?"

She looked meekly at the doctor, attempting to defend her position and the decision she was making to stay in his home. She quietly replied, "Yes, I know. He does drink all the time, and when he isn't drinking, he is smoking pot or doing coke. Last week we got in a bad fight and he told me to get out. He came at me in a drunken rage. He grabs me by the shoulders and shakes me when he gets like that. It got nasty. I snatched my purse and ran out to my car, cursing him as he was shouting filthy words at me.

He chased me out to the driveway and tried to take my keys, but I had already locked myself in the car. As I peeled out, I looked in the rearview mirror and saw his flailing hands punching into the still night air. I drove around for a while, and when I got back to the house, he had locked me out. I ended up with nowhere to go so I spent the night in my car—slept there the whole night, parked on the roof of a nearby building."

She took a deep breath, staring into the distance, and continued, "When I returned home that next morning, he was still drinking and was mad at me. He grabbed me by the throat and pushed me up against the wall, threatening that if I ever disappeared like that again, we were through. He accused me of going back to my old boyfriend's house and sleeping with him. When he finally calmed down, I told him where I had been, and he…well, he seemed to feel bad about it…you know, about how he had treated me."

Within a few days, they were back on Dr. Weatherspoon's couch before Tiffany's next scheduled appointment. She called in frantically; there seemed to have been more verbal and physical abuse, and Tiffany was incapable of speaking clearly, only stumbling to utter her words in a state of fractured confusion. Dr. Weatherspoon found a time slot to get them in for an emergency session.

Even though Sam claimed to love this woman, fully aware and regardless of her traumatic sexual history, he had decided over the past weekend to expose her to the experimentation and proclivities of the local swingers' club. Boasting of his prowess and stamina Sam's exhibitionism seemed to thrill him. Fatefully disastrous and at the expense of Tiffany's already fragile psyche he had convinced her to have sex with him in one of the club's viewing rooms.

Sitting next to this horrid little man, she seemed more broken than ever. Hardly able to utter a cohesive sentence, the words came out in quiet spurts. "Well, um, he said it would please him. I wanted things to be better—you know...between us. I think... I don't know. I thought he would be nicer to me, you know—if I pleased him sexually. It didn't help, though. Sam got super drunk later that night, was snorting, you know—coke, lots of it. We argued again, and um, he got outraged and had his hands around my throat again."

Her body shrunk deeper into the sofa cushions—a visceral attempt to retreat from the man seated near her; her lover, her savior, according to Sam. She let out a sigh and whimpered. "I don't know what he wants or, you know... or even who I am anymore."

Sam was the same man he was eight years ago in his prior therapy. Nothing more than a bully addicted to power, greed, and sex. "I've been with over two hundred women, all kinds, believe me when I tell you that I never lacked for attention in that department," he boasted proudly during their session.

"I'm looking for real love this time, not just what a woman looks like, her age, financial circumstances, or career. I want the real thing damn it, and I thought Tiffany could give me her love in return for what I've done for her. We had a crazy kind of chemistry in the beginning. It seems like it all went to hell when she started on me about my drinking and trying to tell me how to live my life."

"Well, Sam," said Dr. Weatherspoon, "if this is what you call love, I'd hate to see what it would look like if you hated the woman." The doctor wasn't one to verbally dress down her patients unless she felt there was no other recourse. Sam's and Tiffany's self-reports of their abusive physical interactions with each other were beyond dangerous, and potentially lethal.

"Look, Doc, I am not a wealthy man. I live on the top floor of a home that is considered a historical site. Currently, I'm at risk of losing it over some financial complications, and it has been in my family for over one hundred and sixty years. My elderly mom lives downstairs. My money is tied up in this home, and I am my mom's main caretaker. This stress has me running on empty, and the relationship with Tiffany is working on my last nerve, man!" Although Sam cried the blues regarding his circumstances, his wrist sported an expensive Rolex watch and the doctor had seen him step out of a red Ferrari in the parking lot, which sat in full view of the office's large plate-glass window.

"To the public, I look like a respectable and successful man, but the economy is down, and now I find myself supporting Tiff also…I mean, what's a man supposed to do? I'm not goddamned superman! She has a degree and could go back to work, but no…she'd rather play the victim and get high on some ADHD medicine she's been taking for anxiety. Then she gets mad at me and goes behind my back running off to an ex-boyfriend's house for days! I had no idea where she was. I went crazy looking for her without making a scene at work. Her ex works in the same location as I do…It's a real mess, I admit."

In the end, Dr. Weatherspoon's attempts to help this couple failed. She asked Sam during their last session to help place Tiffany in an apartment of her own, and Sam went ballistic. Her reasoning was to provide a buffer between the two of them for a while—a safe house so that she could deal with both finding a job and her sense of self. With that suggestion, Sam shouted at Dr. Weatherspoon, "If you want her in her apartment so badly, why don't I use the money I pay you for her therapy, and squander it on an apartment for her? You haven't helped us a bit, and now you're telling me to let her go?"

Fed up with Sam's all-encompassing disrespect, Dr. Weatherspoon declared her intentions to set this man straight. "Well, Sam, in the first place, I lowered my fee to half of what I usually charge my patients, due to your claimed financial need, and now you're insulting my reliability as your doctor. The issue here is your drinking and battering of Tiffany. Have you forgotten the bruise marks you've left on her neck during your attempts to choke her in a drunken rage and then not remembering it the next morning? I'm advising, if you believe that you love this woman, then you help her gain her independence in order to get well. I'm not asking you to 'let her go.' After all, you don't own her, and she doesn't belong to you. She is an emancipated free woman with an ability to make her own choices in life."

Sam abruptly stood up from the sofa, shouting at and threatening Dr. Weatherspoon. "Don't you dare charge my American Express card ever again for a session! We're leaving!" As he marched toward the exit door, Tiffany rose from the sofa, looking confused and crying. As she headed toward the door in pursuit of Sam, Dr. Weatherspoon took her by the arm to stop her for a moment. "Please feel free to come to see me if you wish. I want to help you and am willing to see you at no charge if you'd like. My door is always open to you."

Dr. Weatherspoon never saw Sam or Tiffany again. As for Sam, the world would have undoubtedly been a better place without him in it. Tiffany's obituary appeared in the newspaper six months after Dr. Weatherspoon had last seen the couple in her office. There was no mention of how she had died, but in a small obscure news article, in lieu of flowers, the family was requesting donations be made to MADD.org. Some media interviews with family and friends reported that she had been pushed to a breaking point in her personal life and felt that her untimely death was most likely a suicide. Tiffany had been an avid sports enthusiast and biker for years. For her to accidently drive off a familiar mountain cliff before dusk, seemed an impossibility to her friends. The unknown outcomes of her patients were the worst for Dr. Weatherspoon. When a patient would basically go off-grid without resolve, there was a sense of loss and helplessness. These were the people and their fall from grace that would haunt Dr. Weatherspoon forever.

9

THE PERSIAN PRINCE

People who are brutally honest get more satisfaction out of the brutality than out of the honesty.

—Richard Needham

Here it was again, the night that many looked forward to with great anticipation—the proverbial night that symbolized the end of the old and celebrated the possibilities of the new. The one day of the year that brings us to the threshold of hopes and dreams of all things possible. A chance for new beginnings, fresh and unadulterated in the coming year. Jane was torn as to what to do for New Year's Eve. Having reconciled the dim choices, in her opinion, of invites and options for the night, she had decided to stay in—though her friend Emily thought it a sacrilege to waste the significant evening. Jane was irritated and feeling pressured as she said to Emily, "Eventful to whom? I know it's New Year's Eve, but I just think there's a lot of pretentious buildup, and it's a grand excuse so that people can throw parties and drink way too much!"

Later that evening tucked into bed and with an hour to go before the ball dropped in New York's Times Square, the phone rang. Not recognizing the number, Jane picked up the phone hesitantly. She thought, *Who would be calling me an hour before midnight? Don't these people have a life, compared to me, who apparently is sitting alone on New Year's Eve?* Reaching for her cell phone, she picked it up with her sunniest voice, barely forcing out a cheerful hello.

"Hello, Jane. It's Cyrus," he said, with a yearning tone in his voice. It was almost a sense of sadness that she heard. "We talked a few weeks ago on Match—I was thinking that perhaps you would want to meet me out for a quick bite to eat tonight, you know, to celebrate the New Year's Eve? I'm out here on the boulevard, just hanging out—I'm looking for a place to get something to eat in all this noise and commotion."

Jane envisioned him wandering up and down the busy downtown main drag, looking for a place to eat. *And now he is calling me to join him, like some sort of a last-minute afterthought.* It seemed rude, not unique—a convenience on his part. After all, she had never even met this man—just one previous conversation and she was expected to show up last minute as his New Year's date – *Oh hell no.* "Well, thank you, Cyrus, but I think I'm just going to stay in for the evening this New Year's" she said as graciously as possible. "Perhaps we can get together during the week and make some plans in advance."

Not really expecting to hear from him again, Jane was pleasantly surprised to get a call the very next day. "Hi there, how was your night? I feel bad about calling you with such short notice last evening, and I'd like to make it up to you. Can I take you to dinner tomorrow night?"

"Actually, lunch would be better. I work late most of this week and have more free time in the afternoons. Does that work for you?"

"Of course," he quickly exclaimed. "Where would you like to meet?"

"Let's meet at the mall. Is Cafe Lux OK with you— say…around one p.m.?"

"Perfect, but I'll be there."

Jane was running late and caught in traffic. She had forgotten about the difficulty of finding a parking place at the mall this time of day. Not wanting to walk a mile in her high heels and unable to find a spot to park, she chose to pull into the valet-paid parking. Hurriedly getting out of the car, she called Cyrus on her cell phone, advising him that she was in the parking lot just a few minutes away.

"Just park," he said gruffly."

She thought to herself, well, that was kind of rude.

Entering the restaurant, she hesitated for a moment in the large lobby, looking around for the man she was supposed to meet. Suddenly she heard her name called. Glancing to her left, seated on the bench, she saw him. It wasn't his face or his stature that she first noticed. It was, instead, those legs of his—muscular and shapely, masculinity exemplified in all its glory. Attached to those magnificent legs was Cyrus, casually attired in a black T-shirt and biking shorts. On any other man, this could have been a fashion-police moment, a complete disaster, but not on Cyrus.

As he stood up to greet her, his presence overwhelmed her. He was a glorious combination of pure sexuality and charisma.

"Oh, you startled me. Why, hello there," she said. With a calm reserve, she could feel her heart pounding as she leaned in for a quick touch-of-the-cheek hello. He stood motionless for a moment, looking down at her with a smile. *Oh my*, she thought, *This man is gorgeous. I'm about to be blinded by those perfect white teeth!* At that moment, the hostess approached them and escorted them to a booth.

Sitting across from Cyrus, they both picked up the menus and were in the makings of attempted small talk, while perusing the lunch specials. Jane made a spontaneous joke about his legs as she accidentally brushed them with the heel of her shoe. "Oh, I'm sorry," she said. "Did I accidentally kick you?"

"Yes, you did, but you can play footsie with me anytime that you'd like," he said, winking at her—weakening her attempts to remain in control of the insatiable lust she felt stirring inside. As they chatted and ate lunch, Jane tried to avert her eyes, looking down into her plate of wild salmon. While the food was delicious, she didn't want to gaze into Cyrus's eyes for too long. She knew for sure that this man was a bachelor who had never been married, most likely a player with the ability to charm the skirt off any woman he so desired.

Lunch came to an end, and he escorted her to the door outside and onto the curb of the restaurant—they stood for an awkward moment until he said, "I'd like to get together again if that's something you would like to do?"

"Well, um, of course, just give me a call…and we can plan something," she quickly added. They parted ways, and she headed to her car, thinking, *Not sure if I'll see him again, but what a handsome specimen of a man!*

Cyrus had advised her that although he lived in the area for pleasure, his business was in the Northeast, and he traveled there every other week, only coming back to town if not hindered by business or his endless quest to travel the world. At first, she had shrugged this off as it didn't seem important at the time. It would only come to matter much later in their relationship, when she genuinely felt the impact and emptiness of the distance between them. His yearly trips to the World Cup soccer, Olympic Games, following NASCAR, running with the bulls in Spain—anything and everything sports oriented and well documented by Cyrus on Facebook—sounded manly and fascinating at first.

The months that lay ahead, however, were to prove to be a merry-go-round straight to hell—disrespectful and vague, Cyrus existed for himself only, a legend in his own mind. A journey that no woman wants to endure, even the modern metro woman; a bourgeois bunch of bullshit anyway, according to Jane. She was a woman with her ear to the ground, aware that most of her women friends had at one time or another confessed to wanting to be in a relationship. They wanted to belong to a man—not owned but belonging in the sense that they mattered and were number one in their man's life.

Although she was lukewarm to his pursuit these days, and indifferent to most of his invitations to get together, they had become lovers. Unable to resist him, a man who knew his birthright to love many women, more than comfortable in the ways of his inherent and cultural seduction, she couldn't help but succumb to his charm.

At first, their tete-a-tetes took as exciting a twist as any could. Jane not wanting to overstay her visit, or worse, be considered some insipid little creature that wanted to curl up in his arms and stay the night. She had laid with him for a short while –

Suddenly noting the time out loud to Cyrus she blurted, "Oh! I must get home. I have to feed my dogs." He had looked at her in disbelief and asked her to stay. "What? I want you to stay with me...I don't want to be alone tonight."

"I'm sorry, Cyrus, but your apartment is an hour away from my home—I'm sure the dogs need to be let out." Jane loved to use her Lab as an excuse when wanting a quick exit from a lover—needing to separate from his environment and settle in for the night in the peacefulness of her own home. Perhaps it was selfish of her in some ways, but in this case, it seemed appropriate that Cyrus was the one now pursuing her, asking not only for her body but to be close to her in the night.

It wasn't until the weeks that lay ahead that she fully understood anything about this man. His business jaunts out of town took him away for weeks at a time, sometimes even a month or so, as his main office was located halfway across the country. As the weeks went on, Jane began to understand that Cyrus was an avid soccer enthusiast. He traveled to all the international games and had even been robbed and beaten up once in one of these foreign countries, yet he still returned to the next international tournament, a relentless fan. No woman would ever be a main priority in his life. Cyrus did just what he wanted to do, for himself. Women were some sort of diversion, objects to be desired and "had "in order to satisfy his insatiable thirst both sexually and for the simple task of conquering what he thought belonged to him.

One evening after a less-than-successful adventure between the sheets, Cyrus lay staring at the ceiling and began to ramble about his life and the women in it. Jane listened, frozen in the moment. It was like a fateful train wreck, but she couldn't draw her eyes away from his face as he went on to talk of a young married secretary with a child whom he had been having an affair with. "Mmpph, I'd like to revisit that, but I don't think it will happen again…she is married with a kid, but man, what a great body."

Jane sat straight up in bed. It was freezing cold out, and the radiator barely warmed the room. Livid now, she hardly noticed the covers had fallen away from her chilled body as she rose to her knees, pointed to the door and yelled at Cyrus to get out of her home. Cyrus looked startled. "What just happened?" he asked; shocked at her demands.

"OMG, you're in my bed recounting fond memories of another woman whom you've slept with!"

"Baby, baby, hold on now…I thought you understood that I have several women around the country and the world for that matter. None of them seem to mind that I have other women. In fact, they are all OK with it. They seem to like the freedom that it gives them."

"What? You're expecting me to believe that your 'other women' know of each other and have absolutely no problem with that?"

"Yes, I swear…that's the truth," Cyrus said with a matter-of-fact tone.

Jane was already halfway across the room and had slipped back into her clothes now. Searching for his, she picked up his jeans and threw them across the bed at him, hitting him in the face. "Get out! Just get out!" she yelled. "I have no time in my life for fools or at least someone who thinks he is a genius yet has the morals of a shark with its eyes rolled back in its head."

"Don't you understand what I'm trying to tell you? I'm being completely honest with you. How can you be angry with me? Are you aware of my situation?"

"What situation?" she asked anxiously.

"I'm polyamorous. I've finally figured it out. I'm telling you that my women know about my other women around the country, and they are good with that. They want the same thing," he pompously stated.

"Yes, you just told me that, but what world do you live in? Are you insane? I don't know of any bright, fully self-esteemed women who would want to share their man!"

Cyrus considered himself to be a "sapiosexual," a term often overused in social networking. Classifying oneself as a sapiosexual meant that you found intelligence the most sexually attractive feature in another person. Clearly seeing himself as above the fray, Cyrus was living in a world of his own creation. Jane, however, wasn't standing for any of his nonsense.

There had been a time where she couldn't get enough of him, craving his body as she had never experienced before, wanting him, tasting him when he crossed her mind. Jane's acupuncturist was worried about her. She explained to Jane that it was Cyrus's male "Jing" energies that had her so riled up and crazy about this man, depleting her of her own female life force. "You need not see this man again," Helen said in her stern Polish voice. "He will be the end of you. It is not healthy to want a man so badly. You are not thinking clearly. You're coming from your root chakra, which is your kundalini vibration, your sexual drive. You need to come from the heart first with a man if it is ever to be anything real. Just look at you. You're completely depleted, weak from this man. You cannot give all of yourself away like that. Don't ever do this again." It would be a few years before Jane spoke to Cyrus again. Even then, it would not be at her making.

Social media is a funny thing when it comes to raising the dead or burying them for all of eternity. One can believe we completely clear ourselves of a past lover, sometimes even forgetting his or her name if need be. Yet in reality in today's world, to hell with '*All of social media*' and its ability to bring these entities flooding back to haunt you; rising from that deep dark place that you've relegated them to, hoping to forget the pain or miseries they've put you through.

"Hi there, it's Cyrus. Would you consider being my lover again?" The message had popped up on her phone late one evening. Jane said hello back, curious to see what he had been up to. She would see his posts on Facebook— pictures of his travels and family—quickly passing over him to the next post, numb and void of any feelings for Cyrus, finally. Now his messages scrolled across her screen, a rapid series of texts, inquiring as to her well-being and status of a relationship.

"Not married yet. I'd love to see you again, and guess what? I've finally figured out who I am and what I want in life, the reasons for why I'm not married."

Taking the bait against her better judgment, Jane typed back, "And just what is it that you've finally figured out?"

"I'm polyamorous! I've continued to see several women at the same time, and it is all going well for me." Jane just couldn't control herself, all her feelings of being taken advantage of and having some odd-at-best status as one of "his women" forced unknowingly upon her. She rattled back, "Oh, and I see that is working out really well for you. You're now forty-seven years old, your family has died, and you're alone in life. No children, no legacy to leave behind. Who will love you and truly be by your side when you're older, when it matters?" She waited...the screen was blank with no response from Cyrus. Attempting to text another message to him, her phone responded with "This person has chosen to not receive messages from you now." *Cyrus had blocked her!*

At first offended and then relieved, Jane was glad to say farewell to the Persian prince and his harem of women. She wondered if he was truly happy, or if he would ever be happy. It seemed he was the black sheep of the family. Cyrus was the playboy, always on the run, perhaps from himself. His career and fortune on the upward climb, yet just falling short of real success, never having lived up to the achievements of his family and older siblings. Perhaps his chosen lifestyle did indeed set him aside as exceeding the average man's existence—at least in his own mind. He had created a world for himself, a distinctive world with no rules for commitment, or dedication to another single human being. A man of wanderlust—that man who marched to the beat of a different drummer.

10

THE LITTLE RED HEN AND THE LONG-LOST LOVERS

Sometimes the questions are complicated, and the answers are simple.

—*Dr. Seuss*

As a newly divorced mother of three, Lorrie had no idea how much of an impact Martha, the soon-to-be nonexistent housekeeper, would make on her life and her future. It had been twenty-five years since the woman had passed through Lorrie's life, yet her words of wisdom peppered both her personal and professional life throughout the years. Martha had stayed on for a brief while after the divorce; however, Lorrie couldn't afford any of the nonessentials she had been privy to as the wife of a prominent lawyer, let alone the superfluous luxury of a nanny/housekeeper.

During the days of post-divorce proceedings, which had been nothing less than brutal, Lorrie looked for a job to no avail. She had been a stay-at-home mother and now found she was alone with three small hungry mouths to feed, all under the age of eight years old. Although the divorce agreement had provided for child support and brief alimony, her ex-husband dragged her through the courts claiming he had no income after a tornado had devastated the downtown business area. Unfortunately, it seemed to be a good-old-boy society in the court system locally; it would cost money she didn't have to pay attorneys to fight for the money rightfully allotted in the final divorce decree. After several go rounds in the court system it was a lost cause. She realized it would be best to get a job and find a way to support herself as a single parent instead of waiting for the divorce courts to do the right thing.

In those final weeks after losing the family home, Lorrie was packing boxes to move herself and the children into a small rental home in the neighborhood. Ron had stopped by to pick up some of his things. He stared at her with cold, glazed eyes and said, "Your family is wealthy. Let them feed you and the children for now. I'm heading off to the Parthenon with a girl I've met."

It would be twenty-five years later until she would fully realize her decision that day to become someone—and it would be the salvation of her life.

Thus, began the journey to go back to school and find her niche in the world. The contents of the house that she could move to the much smaller rental home were packed.

She had found a way to engage the children and give them some hope and expectation that things would be fun in the new surroundings. Only in the nights did she run a bath after the kids were asleep, stepping into the hot steamy water that would muffle the sounds of her sobbing.

Martha came in several days a week to help with the children, as Lorrie was out interviewing for a job, mostly futile attempts. She found intermediate work spraying perfume in a local department store and worried about what would become of her with no formal education and her three babies to care for on her own.

Lorrie always remembered throughout the years what Martha had advised her about men. Whenever Lorrie would consider going out on a date, Martha would always say, "You don't need no woulda, shoulda, coulda man in your life, Ms. Lorrie. He needs to put up or shut up. A good man will bring you flowers and be there for you, no false promises. I'd kick him to the curb if I was you." Martha was small in stature, but a strong and wise black woman who was a part-time preacher in her church. Lorrie gathered her wits about her. Deciding to move on with her life, she had given some thought to dating casually but hadn't found the courage to go through with accepting a one-on-one sit-down interaction "date" just yet. "After all," she told her friends, "I'm not dead, just recently divorced with a solid case of 'jaded-ism'!"

Now, twenty-five years later, Lorrie found herself in conversation with one of her best friends. Vincent was close to her age, a few years older, but had been around the block more than a few times, including five marriages and five ex-wives. She referred to him as her go-to guy, the man she always called when she needed to talk or wanted some solid advice on one thing or another. She seemed to like his laissez-faire attitude about life and the fact that he had street smarts and was savvy.

They had once been lovers, yet now she cherished their platonic friendship, not wanting to go back to where they had once experienced each other physically. Lorrie felt that once you leave a lover, the friendship can grow differently and exist, but she never went backward in time or gave ex-lovers another chance at love. Lorrie had accomplished most everything she had set her mind to over the years. The children were grown and successful, had finished college, and now had families of their own. Things were good, great, even amazing. It seemed that things couldn't get any better now in her life.

While exploring the mountains in Aspen at her youngest son's destination wedding, she suddenly found herself to be in great pain. Thinking it was just altitude sickness that she was experiencing, she tried her best to ignore it for the rest of the trip. After all, she thought, *How could I possibly be sick? I've been working out all summer, joined a gym and was killing myself doing TRX exercises—I'm a damn superwoman, a silly eight-thousand-foot-altitude resort mountain town isn't going to beat me down!*

Lorrie had developed a new admiration and respect for how much oxygen her lungs were capable of acclimating to. At 10,705 feet at the landing peak of Aspen mountain, her son's friends held on to their token groomsmen gifts—little oxygen canisters that were coveted as though they were in possession of some magical potion, gold dust. Fortunately, she had known better than to make that gondola ride up the mountain without first having bought the last handheld oxygen canister at the local drugstore!

Finally, back home, Lorrie went to her doctor to find out why she was still not feeling well. Thus, began a year-long journey, multitudes of doctors, hospitals, medical opinions, misdiagnoses, and all the drama that went along with going through a process of trying to figure out what the hell was wrong with her.

Having always been a brave woman, Lorrie would be tested through this medical journey beyond any boundaries she had ever known. Now about to find out not only what she was truly made of, she was about to embark on a course destined to determine her future. Back and forth between doctors' appointments, scheduled testing, and several exploratory procedures, her world seemed out of control. She said to Hillary, her best friend over the past fifteen years, "How can things go so crazy just as we're rolling along, feeling so invincible, without a care in the world?"

Having experienced a life-threatening illness twenty years ago, Lorrie was no stranger to surviving and beating the odds when it came to the game of life. She couldn't believe she was back facing her greatest fears again; dealing with a medical scare like this brought back the memories and nightmares of having spent several months in ICU those many years ago, almost losing her life to a surgery that had gone so wrong. To have to sit and listen to the droning sound of her doctor's voice—a medical specialist, MD, PhD, a God, in his own right in his field, yet the coldest man she had ever met—was unbearable. She thought, *This is the stuff nightmares are made of.*

Vincent had been a good friend, the kind of man who was generous of heart and caring enough to offer to ride out to the hospital with her on several occasions. Walking into the hospital with her, he looked at Lorrie and said, "This isn't bad. I get good vibes about this place. I've been in hospitals before, and most of them totally creep me out, but this one seems to be OK. I don't get any bad feelings about it."

When Lorrie had first met Vincent, his inordinate ways of seeming to be all-knowing about certain subjects had been intriguing. However, what she had liked about him in the beginning now only served to irritate her. He walked with a cocky stride, his silver-tipped lizard cowboy boots clicking on the freshly polished hospital floors. In his younger days, he had been a real cowboy of sorts involved in military espionage during the Vietnam era, in his midlife years he'd managed several nightclubs in LA and laundered money for the cartels—now a jack-of-all-trades or none.

She was checked in now for the procedure she was to undergo, and they sat together in the waiting area of the radiology department. Lorrie had noticed a young blond girl walk in and sit adjacent to them. Bored to tears, anxious, and frustrated about the lengthy wait to be called in, Lorrie couldn't help but do some people-watching, one of her favorite things when sitting idly by. She wasn't much interested in the blond girl, although Vincent was sizing her up, trying to get her to talk to him. Lorrie could tell by the look on the girl's face that she thought he was as dumb as a bag of hammers. She was slight in build, with short straight blond hair, and otherwise nondescript. Lorrie quickly passed her by to watch an elderly couple—the woman, seemingly his wife, quite ill, and the attentive and caring husband hovering over her, attending to her needs. "Here, honey, drink this down. Yes, that's a good girl," he said gently.

The heavy metal double doors opened, and the nurse called, "Lorrie, Lorrie Hartman?" Lorrie gathered her purse and jacket and promptly obeyed the call from the nurse to enter the cold, long hallway entrance through the electric doors, now closing behind her. It was a menacing feeling. She was entering the bowels of the hospital—the place where life and death happen, one's life dependent upon calculations and numbers, either painting a picture of a hopeful healthy future or an early departure from this lifetime.

Inside the glass-enclosed room, Lorrie carefully laid out her clothes on a chair and locked her valuables in the small locker as the technician instructed her to do. She slipped on the all-too-familiar pale-blue hospital gown and tied it as appropriately as possible so as not to expose too much of her naked bottom.

Somehow this drill had become such a routine in the past few months that she didn't really care if any flesh was showing. Devoid of any sense of vanity at this point, Lorrie walked over to the MRI table. She sat on the edge and assumed the position, straightening her gown as she lay down and was sucked into the claustrophobic vortex of the machine. The technician was kind and asked her if her headphones were adjusted properly so that she could hear the music she had chosen. "Yes, quite good," she replied as the sound of the music drowned out the ominous *thump, thump, thump* of the machine. Quiet now, drifting off in her own mind, eyes closed, she had chosen to just go with the flow and acquiesced to this robotic mind-set to salvage what sanity she had left.

A hymn of sorts repeated in her mind; the words flowed along to the beat of the music coming from her headphones. She had asked the technician for ambient music to help her pass the time in the pounding machine. The words of a pure love, the kind of love that she could count on, surrounded her. She almost felt at peace, realizing that her thoughts were more tangible now than ever. She muffled a laugh that was rising in her throat, as she thought, *nothing like life-and-death circumstances bringing you to the edge of clarity on a quick-zip line! La la la…da da da…*the song repeated in her head. *Hmmmmm.*

I want someone who is real. A man who walks hand in hand with me, not six steps ahead. A man who thinks of me while I'm with him, yet even more when I'm not by his side. A man who can conjure up the taste, scent, and essence of my body and soul…A man who appreciates what and who I am and the journey that I took to become who I am today...A man who thinks I am the most beautiful woman on this earth and doesn't turn his eyes from me to look upon another woman who passes by.

The next week she received an online alert from the hospital with her doctor's report that she had been waiting for. Scared to look but unable to wait until her scheduled appointment, she hesitantly typed in her log-in and password to the medical records link they had sent her. Nauseous from the anxiety, there it finally was in black and white...NEGATIVE. Her heart pounding, she felt the exhilaration and life force of her body pumping through her veins.

Now was the time for a new start for Lorrie. *No more Vincents*, she promised herself. Her sister had rammed it down her throat ad nauseam that if a man couldn't take better care of her than she took of herself, then she didn't need to be with him. It seemed, however, that most of the men, including her ex-husband, were only looking to see what was in it for them. Burned or broke from past marriages, they were either unwilling to give of their heart or had become hardened to the point of brash rudeness. If Lorrie had a dollar for every man who passed her way who was a liar, cheat, cheapskate, married, or had an ex-girlfriend at home or in the trunk of his car, she'd have been a rich woman in the early days of her post-divorce dating.

Hardened now from the long-lost lovers who had so eagerly pursued her over the past years, only to have been disappointed in their carelessness to detail, at times bringing her to low points of not feeling emotionally well, she possessed more than her quota of substantial cerebral wounds for a woman her age. Most of the men seemed to be revisiting some sort of desperate return to their teenage years, wanting to bed everything in sight like boys in a candy store. Rarely did Lorrie come across a man of integrity with any sense of decency or design to authentically want to know her. Perhaps she should have been happy that men desired her, but to be desired for her body without any tribute to her mind was worse than any insult she could have imagined.

All seemed as dark soldiers who had come to force her to choose, darkness or light—perhaps guiding her to who she would become. The hurt, pain, and disappointment with each failed relationship would only serve to make her stronger and more resolute in her mission to become the woman she always knew herself to be—verbally dressed down by a military father, quashed in her speech and aspirations, stringently advised both spoken and inferred: "Be quiet and keep your mouth shut, don't make ripples, why must you always cause trouble?" The words reverberated in her head from a young age. Even her siblings had joined this bandwagon after her divorce and loss of financial means. "You don't deserve…" they would say. "You have to suffer a bit more before you can fly. Who do you think you are?" Unbeatable, Lorrie went on to find her own way in life. Nothing would stop her, not illness, nor hurdles that she could never have imagined.

All paled in comparison to the recent medical fight for her life, to survive.

In the later years of her life, Lorrie had indeed become a successful marketing entrepreneur. Her kids were all grown adults now, successful and with babies of their own. They say that the test of having raised successful children is when they are independent and living their own lives. Although there were miles between them, her youngest son had once said, "Mom, no matter where you are or what you are doing, always remember, at least one of us is always thinking about you." She carried that message close to her heart always.

Men and friends had come and gone over the years. Most wanted something from her, either to share in business endeavors or nudging her to invest in stock options that they had a vested interest in. A whole lot of talk but no action on their parts when she really needed a helping hand—no one to show up at the airport to pick her up from cross-country flights, but still they swore their undying love for her. Her dad had once told her in jest, "Don't love me so much. You're killing me." Lorrie incorporated that line into her repertoire and used it often on her string of long-lost lovers.

One fall evening as Lorrie lay sick in bed with the flu, the winds howling outside, the man of her dreams blew into town with those cold rambunctious winds, ultimately arriving to warm her heart forever. The story was one that she would tell her grandchildren and great-grandchildren one day. She had always known that her man would be a great story. For those whom she left behind in the gray ashes of long-lost promises, she could only be content in their kindred fates as those of the animals in her favorite childhood storybook, *The Little Red Hen*. A prophetic and fitting fate it was. For those who don't help to bake the bread, they cannot ever then expect to partake of the bounty.

11

AMOUR FOU

---

*Sex is the consolation you have when you can't
have love.*

—*Gabriel García Márquez*

In the final days, it was indeed uncontrollable and obsessive passion that ended them. Eduardo's original contact with her had been in a note left on her car windshield. She had noticed him out of the corner of her eye while walking into her agency that cold and windy morning in early March. Unbeknownst to Olivia, he had also taken one glance at her and knew that one day she would be his.

The note had read:

Brains
Beauty
Ballast

You, miss, are high fruit indeed—best we boys skedaddle to Home Depot for a much-longer ladder!

It was his dark and soulful eyes that she had first noticed. They caused her to gasp slightly and catch her breath as he gazed at her in the lunchroom that afternoon. "Who are you looking at? You're in another world and not even listening to what I'm saying," Sherri said in an irritated voice. Sherri was Olivia's secretary and was always on the lookout to find her boss the perfect guy but to no avail.

Tracking Olivia's gaze, she gasped and blurted out, "Oh my, now that is a fine specimen of a man! Tall, dark, and handsome, and he is staring at you with that gorgeous smile!" Eduardo stood out among the masses. How could one not help but notice his focused glances across the cafeteria? Olivia, blushing and embarrassed, tried hopelessly to shush Sherri up, but Eduardo had caught Olivia's eye and knew that she and Sherri were aware of his presence. Sherri was insisting that this was most likely the secret admirer who had so deliciously left the provocative note on Olivia's car earlier that morning. Startled by his voice, they looked up to see him standing before them—owning up to the note so furtively placed on her car window that morning. They exchanged phone numbers, and Eduardo apologized for not being able to have a drink with her later, as his music conference was over and he was leaving town that night.

Olivia hadn't been with a lover for quite some time. Having thought about her predicament of being a

BAV—born-again virgin—she was steadfast in her newly established principle to remain so until she fell in love, for real this time. She knew from a life well lived that sex with indiscriminate lovers was easy; it was intimacy that was a bitch. For Olivia, honestly engaging with another in the fine details and nuances of relationship and love meant willingly surrendering herself to the possibility of delight and happiness, or in the long run, devastation.

He had called her that evening, and every evening since then. Olivia looked forward to his calls, feeling closer to him with every conversation.

They satiated their lust for one another over the phone with endless nights of sexting…and fantasy. She wanted him desperately, and desire was overriding any sense of reason. She could think of no other man, and her yearnings would not be quenched until they could get to each other's side and finally lie tangled in each other's arms.

He had advised her in the beginning that his time was limited and divided, dedicated to his work, his young children who lived with him, and his colleagues who worked on his musical projects. Finally coming back into town for business, they consummated their lust at an out-of-the-way bed-and-breakfast, far from the maddening crowds of the big city. Knowing that she only had him for the night, Olivia desired more than a one-night stand. Sex and lust often cloud the mind, and the body wants what it wants in those decisive moments. She took him as her lover, and in his absence, she could taste him on her lips whenever he crossed her mind.

Waking to his texts each morning for the first week after they had first been together—

"Hello sexy." At first, she had thought these messages a flattering connection, their little sweet thing between them only. As she picked up the phone and read his text, she stretched her body beneath the warm sheets in the morning sun filtering through the windows. She couldn't help but be excited when thinking of him, now feeling the sexual stirrings in her groin—like little bursts of pre-orgasmic explosions when reliving his touch, the feel of his hands and mouth on her flesh. The sex between them reminded her of her first lover after she had divorced in her twenties.

Eduardo knew how to touch her—he moved her body as though he was handling the wheel of a race car as she climaxed on top of him and writhed with pure pleasure. He wasn't a selfish lover yet was anxious to enter her again. Lying back on the pillows, he pulled her on top of him again. Reluctant in her post-orgasmic sedated state to 'go for it again', she however obliged and straddled him, now eagerly sliding onto his hard cock. "No," he said, looking into her eyes with his hands firmly placed on her hips. "Don't move and let me do it." He was fucking her now in a rhythmic motion, asking her if she could orgasm simultaneously with him. "Are you OK?" he asked, still plunging into her without slowing down.

It was a mixture of pain and pleasure, and yet she obligingly whispered, "Yes, oh yes." Hoping it would be over with soon, worried that her treasurable clit would be crushed from his thrusting and disintegrate into oblivion at any moment.

"Cum with me...cum with me..." he moaned. "Tell me when—"

"Now, oh now," she said, pleased that she could pleasure him so, but desperate for the assault of his ten-inch manhood to subside. *I always could fake a great orgasm*, she thought to herself as she slid off him and lay curled in his arms. He was a sensual and skilled lover, possessing the nuances of knowing just how and where to touch a woman. Not pressing his full body weight against her, he firmly grasped her small delicate wrists and pressed his mouth into the small of her neck, moving down to her breasts. Never losing his concentration, he made love to her body as though it was covered with caviar until she was lost in the ecstasy of his tongue.

Was it merely that she knew he was only here for a few fleeting moments of pleasure that prevented her from falling into the vulnerability of that sweet orgasmic out-of-body feeling? This man was a good lover, yet sex was just not enough. For Olivia, without the connection of the most profound kind of sex, sex with full-blown intimacy, sex with a man that wanted to know her in every way possible, both in and out of bed, an orgasm was rarely forthcoming. Olivia drifted into the quiet moments that passed. Surrendering to the strong, safe curve of his shoulder, she was content in the calm aftermath.

Finding yourself facing the reality of your relationship is usually a bad sign of things to come. The mere fact that you got to that place in your head—replaying the details from beginning to present and wondering, "What's wrong here?"

Eduardo had advised her up front, that he merely wanted to be with her sexually, an exciting, almost elicit exchange of bodies for sexual pleasure only. This alliance would have its boundaries, though—no dating, no relationship, no having to answer to each other. Yet ultimately it would end in a friendship one day. He had also told her there had been another time in the past when he experienced this type of acquaintance with a woman, just one single other time in his life— and that the sex was the best he had ever had.

Olivia was in a place of transition in her life. Ordinarily, she would have scoffed at such an offer of "friends with benefits." This axiom was so clichéd now, it had become a phrase listed in the Urban Dictionary. It must be real! She mockingly laughed when she found it there. It was a label for those who were willing to hook up with no intimacy or rules, a toss between the sheets void of any human or emotional civility.

Olivia was no fool and indeed not the type to be taken advantage of. However, she had no patience for dating, and the thought of even "looking for a relationship" sent shivers up her spine. She would rather sit in the dentist's chair than endure one more lousy date. She felt in conflict with herself over wanting him and experiencing the lust between them, and yet wanting to be fully present and engaged in a whole relationship with a man—this always seemed to elude her.

They had broken it off after their last tryst together. Eduardo had insisted that Olivia had ruined it by attempting to define what they had. When she had exclaimed that she needed a one-to-one relationship, one where there was respect and no hints of his other women, he stated, "If you expect me to follow you around like a puppy dog with his tail between his legs, I think you're sadly mistaken. You just don't get me."

"No—I guess I don't get you. You joke around that you love to love women and that after your divorce you are now glad that it happened. You've never given me any indication that you wanted to 'date' me...I only hear you calling me for a booty call and wanting to fuck me. For some women that would be enough, but for me, it is just a few moments of pleasure and then feeling empty afterward." She asked, "Are you seeing other women?" "You don't really want the answer to that question, now do you?"

It had been over a month since she had heard from him. On this lazy winter afternoon, he called and said he was an hour away. He worked across several state lines with his musical career, and she never knew when he might be in the area. He asked if he could see her, and she complied with his request. After all, shouldn't they be able to enjoy each other, pleasure each other without any societal judgment? They were both consenting adults. These words ran through her head as she scurried around, straightening up the house and the bedroom. So, what if I want to be in his arms again, have him make wild love to me?

He was one of the only men who could make her feel the way she did when they were together. Differentiating between the sexual lust and standing by her moral resolve was a battle she realized she wasn't winning. Having joked with him often on the phone while they weren't seeing each other, she had informed him that she and her vagina, which she had graced with the name Jane, were at great odds. Jane wanted to see him desperately, but Olivia said, "Hell no!"

He had not been in her bedroom before. It was her sacred place, bright and airy with dark wood floors and white stucco walls. She had chosen this loft for its soaring ceilings and the abundant space for her easel, art materials, and numerous paintings—many unfinished, as her career seemed to stand in the way of her passion for her art.

This was her creative sanctuary, and to let a man into her private space meant something special to her. Climbing up into her four-poster bed where he had comfortably settled in, she asked him how his day was. The lights were low, and she couldn't see his eyes, but he sharply answered, "Can't we just enjoy the moment? I don't want to ruin it with conversation."

Although Eduardo was a fantastic lover and pleased her immensely when she could just let go... in an attempt to numb her mind— yet the truth blared at her like a thousand horns. She was always looking—no, hoping—that he would break free from the frozen guard that he wore like a badge and utter a straightforward word to her that wasn't some sexual cliché like "If I can get hard again, I'm going to fuck the hell out of you." Not exactly what her heart longed for—and it was sad that she even thought this man could ever be anything other than what he was.

However, this time he had asked to look into her eyes while they were making love. "I want to see you, this is better, isn't it?"

He kissed her passionately and seemed differently connected to her, holding her tightly. He finally released her and sat up to get dressed. Normally their times together were brief. Standing up he grabbed his jeans off the chair and then sat down on the leather ottoman next to the bed. Leaning over her, he suddenly buried his head in her chest and nuzzled her, kissing and playfully biting her forearm. He laughed and said, "Wow…I just went off on your forearm."

"Oh, I forgot to tell you," she said. "You know the lab results I was worried about? I heard from my gynecologist, and he said I'm fine, just overworked and probably needing a vacation. The doctor laughed when I told him I was freaked out about being exhausted at spin class. He said the test results were perfect and that I'll probably live to be one hundred and eleven years old!" She knew she was risking going into the territory of reality, which he did not like. He replied, "Well then, I can marry you now and then kill you off and seize all your money." She looked at him, shocked by his statement, not even capable of truly believing that she had heard him correctly. It seemed to Olivia as though they were both frozen in time, and everything was moving in slow motion.

Suddenly Eduardo spoke breaking the awkward silence. "It's funny, you know—I've never really dated an older woman before." She was aware of his attempts at severe mind-meddling. As she teasingly slapped him and laughed at his comment, she thought, *Why do men need to play this?* Eduardo was forty-two, and Olivia was forty-five. She was at the top of the career ladder, and aware of her accomplishments and personal evolvement, it was nearly impossible to quell her fire. Olivia had carved her sense of self-worth in stone.

After he had kissed her goodbye and departed on his road trip to another out-of-state gig, she couldn't get that brief sweet moment she had seen in his eyes out of her mind. This was Olivia's Achilles' heel, her weak spot for having faith in people and wanting to believe they had the same sense of decency and honor as her.

It was this tendency to want to be the Velveteen Rabbit, to love and to be loved so hard that your little cotton nose was almost rubbed off—only then, at that moment, fully realizing that you had become real! Damn that childhood fairy tale that had led her to believe such love existed and that continued to lead her as an adult down that same corridor toward the destruction and disappointment of her hopes and dreams. "Just stop it," she heard herself talking out loud. She did this often when in an internal fight with herself. It seemed to clarify the confusion in her head. Going from hating him to longing for his touch, she inherently knew the answer to her indecisiveness and the choices she had to make.

The summer passed quickly. It felt like years since she had seen him. Every morning in the first week or so, she would receive a text—not even a few simple words but rather a superficial "GM." She thought nothing of it at first, rushing around to get dressed for work with a bowl of oatmeal in her left hand and a slice of buttered toast in her mouth while looking for the matching pair of the boots she wanted to wear that morning. Only on those weekend mornings when she could lie languidly between the crisp sheets did it dawn on her that he never actually said anything to her. Nothing but his perfunctory GM's. She began to believe those messages were probably sent out in one bulk text message to his entire lineup of women.

It was now August, with no respite from the unbearable heat. Olivia's morning swims were more of a wet one-hundred-degree sauna than a relaxing, meditative time-out. Her thirty laps across the pool relaxed her, and her mind seemed to clear in the turquoise water, the heat enveloping her body and her soul.

She noticed a message on her phone as she walked to the chaise lounge to retrieve her towel. Ignoring the text, she went on with her day. She was angry with him. He seemed to treat her as an afterthought, not how she expected to be in a man's mind if she had ever really mattered to him.

Out to dinner with a man she had met at her CrossFit class, she heard a text bleep on her phone. She and Eduardo were not exclusive. He had made it quite clear that he didn't care if she dated other men, as long as she didn't sleep with them. Those discussions were in her mind, the final blow to her self-respect. Yet she continued to see him whenever he showed up. "Hello," he had texted her after being off the radar for over a week now. Not having physically laid eyes on him since early June, as he spent the summer in Colorado, she was anxious to see if he was back in town.

She waited until she had a free moment and responded, "I'm on a date."

"Well, it doesn't matter, because you know you're thinking about my cock. I've ruined it for you—you know you'll be thinking of me all night now while you're with him."

By the mere fact that Olivia had responded to his text, it was immediately apparent to her that she wasn't interested in her date at all. She took a moment when he had excused himself to use the restroom to answer Eduardo. Knowing it to be a shady move, and somewhat disappointed in herself, she ignored her inclinations to be honorable and respectful to the poor unsuspecting man whom she was with.

She quickly texted back, "Yes, you most likely have ruined my evening with this man, but that doesn't mean I'll be seeing you again. If anything, I am more determined than ever to end whatever was between us." She was missing a piece of the puzzle with Eduardo. Not knowing how she felt about him anymore, she would lean on her male friend's shoulders and pour out her heart—a dangerous source of advice most often, as her male friends had their own vested interests in Olivia.

He had once said that when they were together, she had his full attention. That statement had made her feel compartmentalized—only fitting into his life when it was at his convenience. He was a Ken-doll situation now, clearly lacking that "manning up" fierceness that she so badly needed in a man. Her guy friends would say, "Make sure he brings his vagina with him on your next date." They knew he wasn't giving Olivia all of himself, only a little plastic doll in the box that all little girls wanted to make a perfect match for their picture-perfect Barbie.

His past marriage was a vague mystery, other than he had told her once that his ex-wife had left him for another man. She hadn't dug any further into it, figuring that he would tell her the details when they knew each other better.

Torn and fractured by the frustration of his distancing and haphazard attention to her, she still couldn't put this thing to rest with Eduardo. Late that Saturday night she Googled his name again—having found nothing much of interest the first time she had done so months before. Something in her, perhaps it was her own intuition prodding her to investigate further— looking for some clues to who this man was. This time, she came across an online site that verified identities, and under his name were listed "possible relative." She saw a woman's name, "Tatiana Foucault," with his last name, listed as a relative. Figuring this must be an ex-wife she wondered if there was anything about her—a picture maybe, an address...she clicked on the hyperlink.

The shock of what she saw took a minute or two to settle in. Feeling as though she had just been kicked in the belly, she read in horror and disbelief, the national media headlines about this woman's arrest and criminal conspiracy charges in Washington, DC, for allegedly attempting to sell blood diamonds from Africa along with her several co-conspirators. Purporting to be from a royal bloodline from Romania, the Duke of Vlach having reportedly been in her genealogy, she ostentatiously carried the prefix "Duchess" to her name.

It appeared that Duchess Tatiana Foucault was now deemed a faux aristocrat and had been blackballed from her previous life of hobnobbing with high society in Washington.

Though she was only found guilty of misdemeanor charges and received three years' probation, the mere thought of Eduardo's association and ten-year past marriage to this woman made her cringe. Still she shuddered in disbelief, stunned at this tell-tale dirt on Eduardo's ex-wife.

That old saying "The apple doesn't fall far from the tree" applies also to who you're dating! One of Olivia's professors had once said, "Show me who your friends are, and I'll tell you who you are."

None of this sordid history had ever come up for discussion in the several months she had known Eduardo. His only mention of her had been one evening on their third dinner date when Olivia had first asked about his ex. "My ex?" He looked uncomfortable as he said, "She left me when I ran into financial problems during the market crash. I had promised her a good life, and I let her down."

"Oh my, that's awful!" Olivia proclaimed. "Is she OK now? Whatever happened to her? What kind of woman would do such a thing?" she asked compassionately, feeling somewhat sorry for him at that precise moment. He replied, "Well, she has several children from a past marriage. Her first husband was Greek and very wealthy. She went back to him with the children."

"Oh...OK. Well, sounds like she was only a good-time woman, staying with you only when you could provide her with a certain lifestyle." "Well, as I said, I let her down." There was something tragic about him—something lonely. They never discussed his past again in those early on-again, off-again months of dating. That is until Olivia, once again, listened to her female knack of knowing and had the good sense to Google, her indiscriminate lover.

She was having this plethora of Internet information weighing on her for days now, and against her better judgement, she hastily picked up her cell and called him. Confronting Eduardo, she asked him if he had been involved. "Oh, my God," he blurted out, "Not this again. My last girlfriend was obsessed with this. None of that was true. The press took what had happened and blew it out of proportion. She truly did have royalty in her bloodline. We were madly in love in the beginning. She was beautiful, you know. When we got divorced, she got involved with some bad people. They are the ones who got her involved in all that stuff."

Eduardo seemed unsettled and said, "I'm going take a rain check on that dinner date for Saturday. I think I'll just go for a ride and figure some things out for myself." Floored by his statement, Olivia questioned him,

"What are you talking about? Because I asked you about your ex-wife, you're breaking our date?" He answered, "Why are we even having dinner?" And there it was—instead of apologizing to Olivia and asking her to understand that he wasn't responsible for his past wife's moral compass and illegitimate business involvements, he aggressively defended her and broke their date. For Olivia, there was no going back now. Eduardo had clearly shown his allegiance to a woman from his past; a mere phantom.

They met one last time. Agreeing to meet him for lunch on Halloween day, fitting to the situation, a cynical twist to their inevitable demise. They met at the quaint organic café where they had dined on eggs Benedict on their first date. His face looked apprehensive; his skin as pale as the egg whites against the gray sheen of the ceramic plates. Gazing directly at him, she could see right through him. More than anything, she felt sorry for him. Why hadn't she seen before that this man was a wounded bird, sensitive, and fractured by life? But naïve to the exploits of his ex-wife? No way. To Olivia's chagrin, she knew in her heart that he was crooked; mindlessly collaborating in the tainted connections of his ex-wife's scandalous pursuits.

Olivia never saw him again. Their insatiable passion for each other had no chance of surviving the greater pain that Eduardo was to carry in his heart eternally. Sex and lust are never enough to endure the most benign rigors of relationship; indeed, not the twisted and thorny trails that this man wandered hopelessly through. Eternally guilty in his own mind of letting down his past love, "the Duchess," never climbing to the financial heights of security and lifestyle that he had promised her. Some never break free from the voices in their heads, and their self-inflicted measures of failure in love and life.

12

RODEO COWBOY

Come quickly—as soon as these blossoms open,
they fall. This world exists as a sheen of dew
on flowers.

—Izumi Shikibu

He had gone out looking for trouble that wet and stormy August evening. A widower now for five years, he had in the past frequented the country bars to dance and be picked up by women. He didn't have to work at it at all. Couples often approached him for a night of swinging, and he was happy to oblige. He had described it to close friends, both male and female, as "an easy way to hook up without doing all the work."

"Why not?" he said proudly. "If a man wants me to service his beautiful wife, why on earth would I turn that down? I mean, it's usually wealthy couples where the wife is younger and gorgeous, and the husband just wants to keep her happy." Now, however, he was older and claimed to have changed his ways. To look at him, no one would have guessed that Roy was in his early sixties. Hard bodied with words as smooth as a good whiskey, he still had that something special that made the women surrender to his charm. Not looking to swing now, he was still pure sex on a stick. No relationship could survive this man. Honesty and commitment eluded him, and nothing but trouble came from any liaison with this cryptic dude. He was six foot three and sporting a 10X Stetson.

Roy was an unusual figure of a man who stood out from the crowd. Once he set his focus on a woman, she was soon to be putty in his hands.

He had been married once at a young age. Two children were born from that fated connection. Though it seemed the right thing to do at the time, the children grew up without knowing their father. He had been there for their early birthdays and then seemed to lose touch with them as they entered their teenage years. Never knowing the damage, he had done to their young psyches, he was now viewed by his grown children as a self-centered, narcissistic waste of skin. It did not matter to him, as he had long ago written them off as spoiled ingrates.

She was sitting at the bar, eating roast-beef sliders and drinking ginger ale. He had noticed her from across the room since she was one of the few good-looking women in the bar who was minding her own business and chowing down on her food, ignoring all advances from the cowboys who had dared to approach her. Small in stature but strikingly beautiful, on that evening she was in a world of her own. "Hello, sweet thing," he said, the words syrupy as he gave her his best smile. "Mind if I sit here next to you and keep you company? Someone has to protect you from all these badass men devouring you with their eyes."

"Suit yourself," Priscilla said as she briefly glanced at him but quickly returned her attention to her food.

Stunned by her cold reception to his charm, he purred, "Now, baby doll, what is going on with you? You're too darn pretty to be sitting here all alone. C'mon, baby, don't ya want to be my girl?" Not in any mood at all to be sweet-talked by this old fool, she nonetheless found his smile and sky-blue eyes warm and inviting. His persistence was both annoying and comforting at the same time. He reminded her of her Louisiana roots and the folks she grew up around.

A real Southern upbringing leaves its mark in more ways than one can imagine. That old saying, "You can take the girl out of the South, but you can't take the South out of the girl"—Well, it's for darn sure the truth, she thought as she finished up her meal with "Old Blue Eyes" still sharing the barstool next to her. Ordinarily, by this point, she would have told him straight up that she was trying to eat and would be more than happy to talk to him later—not likely to happen, but her way of not being totally rude when trying to tell a guy to buzz off.

He was telling her how he had been raised by his grandparents, handed off to them by his mother at a young age, and worked on their farm along with the rest of the hired help. His upbringing had been rough, but he said it had made him the man he was today, a self-made man, raised up by his own bootstraps—a saying that Priscilla had heard before as a young girl. She was pretty sure it had been voiced by her own mother who had heard it from Pricilla's grandfather. She was a second-generation Russian American. The saying was undoubtedly reflective of what her great-grandparents had gone through, arriving in this country as children of immigrants, and having to find their way in life. She could hardly imagine the language barriers and what they must have gone through as children and eventually parents, having to make a living in an unexperienced, foreign culture.

Her heart softened in the moments of his story. She thought to herself, *I'm feeling something for this man; not sure though if it's pity or attraction.* Perhaps it was something close to admiration for what he had survived as a child, yet a sense of numbness and sad sentimentality made her throat feel tight as she listened.

The boy had been given away to his grandparents at such a young age—not to be brought up in a life of luxury, but recruited unwillingly by the plantation owner, his grandfather, to work the land as another farmhand. This had left an indelible mark on Roy, both good and bad. The fact that he had survived his cruel and lonely childhood and had succeeded in both life and business, warranted something, if not absolute respect.

"C'mon, sweet thang…you going to tell me what your beautiful name is? He asked coyly, flashing that big broad smile at her. The whole cowboy thing didn't hurt either. She was entirely over the local guys in their $5,000 suits and $2,000 ties. It seemed that they were all mortgage poor and complete phonies when it got down to the nitty-gritty of who they were. Most had hit the wall by age fifty and lost it all to either their poor choices in business or their ex-wives.

Pricilla's best friend Helen would eternally claim, "All the good men are married." Refusing to believe that blanket statement or euphemisms of "*all*" of anything in life. For Priscilla, her optimistic belief and seeing life not as black and white but rather "gray," meaning that anything and everything was possible if only your mind-set and attitude were in the right place, carried her through her life's journey now.

She was not as optimistic as the cultish law-of-attraction people but confident enough to have achieved many of her goals without having let the hurdles along the way beat her down. Perhaps that's why she tended to give people whom she met second and even third chances, even if they disappointed her along the way.

She glanced over at Roy, really looking at him this time. Although he was charismatic in a vague kind of way, there was something homegrown about this man. "I live up in the mountains of Colorado. Have myself eighty acres on the riverfront, the Silver Snake Ranch...It's really something, baby. You've just got to see it. Water rights are what it's all about. I'm in town visiting for a while, completing the purchase of some ranch land I bought...forty acres, not as big as my other property but damn warmer than the Colorado winters and prettier with the lake and all. I'm going to build me a nice home out there with a wraparound porch to sit out on in the mornings while I'm drinking my coffee. There are ducks out there now, but I'm damn sure putting some swans in that lake for you, baby. They'll remind me of just how beautiful you are. Maybe you can come out and visit me there when it's finished. I'm sure you can get some work done out on my front porch, in the peace and quiet of the ranch."

Pricilla picked up the red checkered cloth napkin from her lap and wiped the corners of her mouth ever so carefully to not miss any of the barbeque sauce on her chin. Carefully placing the napkin on the counter, she swiveled in her barstool so that she was facing Roy directly, eye to eye. "You just want to come in and kiss and bang...Do I look like I was born yesterday? Is there a big 'All seducers, phonies, and players, come right this way' sign on my forehead?"

"My, oh my, girlie, what is up with that?" Roy seemed legitimately taken aback by her tone of voice and accusations. Pricilla snapped at him again. "You can't be putting your hands on the small of my back, and cozying up to me like you own me," she said firmly. "A man needs to earn the right to touch me and properly speak to me. You just can't be taking liberties that you have no right to."

"I'm so sorry, baby, please let me make it up to you and let me show you a great night when I get back into town next month," he said. Attempting to appeal to her soft side, he continued, "I do declare, I think you are one handful of a woman. Anything you say, sweetheart. Just please give me a chance to prove myself to you. I'm frustratingly fascinated by you."

Pricilla had been feeling alone and down over the past few months. The holidays had come and gone, and she had spent most of them on her own. Before she answered him, she thought, it would be nice just to have a good friend, have some time off, and hang out on a beautiful ranch for a few days. Maybe I'll consider it down the road. First, let's see what this man is made of. If he is who he says, I'm sure he'll be able to run to the head of the pack.

"I'll have to think about it. OK. What would you like to do? It's up to me." Priscilla, suddenly realizing that she had misspoken, meaning only to consent to Roy's offer as a gesture of feminine guile, broke into hysterical laughter.

Roy bounced the statement back at her and said, "Yes, you're right. It is up to you!" They both laughed as he teased her about the Freudian slip of the tongue. "It's always up to the woman. I don't know why you women pretend to play the subservient position with us men. If a man has half a brain in his head, he always knows to try and please his woman." He walked her to her car and took her hand in his. Raising her long, perfectly manicured fingers to his lips to impart a good-night kiss, he leaned in and whispered in her ear, "Good night, baby doll, I'll be in touch."

As the weeks went by after their meeting at the Continental Dance Club & Bar, Roy called Pricilla almost every day. If it wasn't a phone call, it was texts and pictures of the barn and home that was being built on his newly acquired property. The lake was as beautiful as he had promised, and the house was coming along quickly. He said the architect was working on the final details of the floor plan. The construction of the main home was to begin soon. Always attempting to include her in the ongoing process, he would tell her how he could imagine her sitting out on that wraparound porch in the late evenings with him, sharing the beauty of nature and each other's company.

Flowers arrived weekly; usually white long-stemmed roses, wrapped in lovely green and gold paper, neatly tucked and tied in the crisp elongated white boxes that the deliveryman left on her doorstep. One might have thought that Priscilla had won the lottery. The FedEx trucks also pulled up to her driveway each week, with boxes filled with everything from cowboy hats and riding boots to the smallest of gifts that sparkled and glimmered but were also way too expensive to accept. Her notes back to him read, "Please, Roy, although I appreciate the sentiment, you must stop sending me expensive gifts. I've insured them and returned the jewelry to you. I just can't accept gifts of that nature from you. We hardly know each other."

The more Priscilla stood her ground and refused to submit to Roy's declaration of his feelings for her, the more he upped the stakes. His gifts always included a handwritten note, stating, "Yes, baby doll, I know, but you're going to be my wife one day."

The texts and photos and gifts continued for the month he was away. He asked Priscilla to find him a hotel near her home. It would make it convenient for him. He was planning on flying in from Colorado to check on the status of the construction of the ranch home and would then drive down so that he could finally see her again.

Several days later Roy arrived in town. Priscilla drove to meet him at his hotel. She had selected one of the more upscale hotels in the area, but not the most expensive. Not wanting to make a choice for him, she wondered whether he would choose luxury or price-saver lodging. She had sent him several links and left it up to him to select the hotel that best suited him. She thought, *Hmm...well, at least he seems to have some idea of a higher standard of living...if he knew to stay in the local boutique hotel, new and modern, on the water and with a restaurant on the premises.* Ambiance was important to Priscilla following too many years of cheap and seedy dates.

The St. Piedmont was an upscale historic hotel with charm and class. She didn't want him to pick her up at her home, still unsure of exactly who this man was. As she drove into the valet, he was already standing downstairs in a turquoise western-style shirt, wearing his Stetson. "Come on," she said, "I'll drive since I know my way around this city."

"No way, ma'am. I'm the man. I'll drive. C'mon and get on up in my truck." Unaware for the moment that this suave bola cowboy had her in some sort of trance, she obeyed his demand as he opened the door for her and helped her step up into the F-350 Ford truck.

As they walked into the restaurant, Priscilla noticed that the patrons were staring at Roy and his cowboy getup. She didn't care what other people thought in this town. Knowing that a person is more than his or her outer appearance, she wanted to know more about this man. He was not her type in any form or fashion, yet he had her attention. "You know, baby, my back is killing me. I've got to go on out to the car and get myself my pain medication. You wait right here now...Why don't you go ahead and order?" Walking back into the restaurant from the parking lot, Priscilla could see from afar that his gait was that of a man in pain. With a slight limp to his left leg, he managed his way over to the table and slid in across from her.

Looking at him again, even more closely now after not having seen him for so long, she realized he was big and bulky, nothing like she had remembered him from when their first met. The conversation was a diatribe of old war revelations, of his younger years as a police captain. As his voice droned on, Priscilla twisted in her seat. How had she let this go so far? Wanting to run but knowing she had allowed Roy to come to town to see her, she was sentenced to the day and evening with him.

Taking an incoming call to her phone, she simultaneously brushed a pesky fly away from her face. It had seemed odd that in such an upscale restaurant the staff would not have noticed the nasty little pests on the premises. Now the fly had landed on Roy, taking flight and coming back in again for another landing as his large rough hands swatted it away. She had visions of a scene out of some old exorcist film and got a chill up her spine. Perhaps this man was a messenger of Satan. Her luck with men lately hadn't been good—it wouldn't have surprised her if the devil himself was sitting across from her.

Roy seemed to be in a great deal of pain and suggested going back to the hotel for a short rest. "I'm in some really terrible pain, baby. Can you help me up to my room and keep me company for a while?" He went into the bathroom and came out in a change of clothes, now dressed in an orange shirt and shorts and socks, getting into bed and motioning for her to come over and sit with him. Pulling her close he asked her if she loved him and would she marry him, insisting that he would take care of her and give her a good life. Could this man be for real? Surely, it was just a poor attempt to get her into bed. "I'm going take you to a place downtown, baby, tomorrow, and you'll love it."

"Oh, a restaurant you're fond of?" Pricilla uttered, waiting for whatever fiasco he had come up with now.

"No, baby, a place that I rent out for the night, just you and me. You're going to love it—and you're going to call me daddy, baby. Daddy's gonna take good care of his baby girl."

She felt him drift off with his arms still wrapped around her. Feeling trapped in the heat of his body, Roy finally let go his grasp of her hand and rolled over. Facing the wall with his back to her, he began to snore, drifting into a deep sleep. Making sure that she had her sunglasses, purse, and keys to her car, she leaned over to make sure that he was indeed asleep, and then quietly super sleuthed it out the door, trying to make the least noise possible so as not to wake him.

Walking quickly to the elevator, she had the most awful feeling that if she turned around, he would be running up behind her asking where she was going. Quickening her pace, she pressed the elevator button and swiftly entered. As she turned to face the hallway, all was clear. She had pulled off the perfect exit, escaping without any confrontation. She headed out of the hotel lobby, her heels clicking on the marble floors until finally, *ahhh*...the heat of the night air enveloped her, and she finally felt safe climbing up into her SUV. *What was that? I totally just "ninjaed out" on the guy! Apparently, my natural reasonings are trying to tell me something is amiss here!*

She thought for sure that she would hear from him later that evening, although truly hoped that she would never hear from him again. The next morning, she rang his room, calling to see if he felt any better. There was no answer...She called back about thirty minutes later to ask the front desk. "Why, Mr. Waterstone checked out about an hour ago." Priscilla was now listening to the receptionist but hearing her words as if in a slow-motion fog and attempting to make sense of what she had just heard. "OK, thanks," she said, hanging up the phone quickly and dialing Roy's cell phone.

"Hi there, I just called the hotel to see if you were OK since you weren't feeling well last evening, and they said you checked out."

"I did. You showed me your true self, and that's all I had to know."

"What on earth are you talking about? I left without wanting to wake you, as I knew you were in a lot of pain from your back."

"Yeah, well, I asked you to marry me, and you snuck out in the night, leaving me to wake up alone this morning. I checked and saw that you hadn't taken my wallet or jewelry. Still, though, I'm heading home. You can stick a fork in it. This is done. You've shown me everything I needed to see."

An old friend of Priscilla's, a director of communications for the city police department, had once told her that sometimes you just can't win for trying. A caring heart often begets callous indignant usury. Her friend had also advised her that if you try to figure out what someone else is thinking and why they do the things they do; you'll drive yourself crazy. Some things are just not meant to be understood. Somehow, though, she knew she had missed the bullet on this one—something to be thankful for... never to have laid foot on the Silver Snake Ranch.

13

It suddenly dawned on him that he had never
stopped to realize, he was alive –

—Unknown author

J oe had once been a figure of success in his heyday. Having fallen victim as so many had during the housing bubble and financial crisis during 2008, he had never gone back to work in that field again. That's all she knew of him as that was all he had told her about his career—referring to himself as "retired now." It was usually jargon for being unemployed. Married once at an early age, Joe now considered himself a bachelor. It seemed to him that he had never really been married. Admitting to mechanically signing papers once when he was twenty-one years old—the marriage lasting only fourteen months. They had been two hopeful young souls who had bought into the stereotype of love at first sight. He didn't consider himself to be bitter. Yet he had never put himself out there emotionally; not wanting ever to be entirely responsible for another person again.

Standing outside on his front driveway, he saw Sylvia coming down the street and waved her in. They had agreed to get together for some coffee and conversation and Joe had promised to show her the abundant literary collection he was so proud of.

The week before, they had met by backing into each other in the narrow aisle of the bookstore. Joe had done a double take and had a hard time believing that he would have such good luck. This kind of thing only happened in the movies. Embarrassed and laughing they intro-duced themselves to one another, realizing they were both searching for a newly released book from the same author. Sylvia thought it a sort of kismet moment that Joe was reading the same book that she had begun a few weeks ago. They were both book lovers, a dying breed, and she was captivated by this tall stranger. Not one to yield to mesmerism, she was taken in by his intellectual and temperate banter.

Joe approached at a steadfast gait. Once at her side, he leaned in and kissed her gently on the mouth. Sylvia wasn't offended by his forwardness. Although they hardly knew one another, she felt instantly at ease with him and allowed him to escort her into his home.

A home can always tell you something about who a person truly is. Not only the furnishings and artwork, but the general feel of the house speaks loudly to one that is aware of such things. Sylvia had always felt that she was a bit of an empath, able to sense people's emotions, even having often attributed feelings to inanimate objects as a young child. She remembered once that she had brought her toy shovel in from the cold one winter day. It was blue and had a smiling face on the handle. She had placed it in her doll's bed where she imagined it would be safe and warm. Realizing her unique sensibilities, yet never thinking them odd, those sensory traits had continued throughout the years.

Joe kept his home quite orderly, neat, clean and void of clutter. Not one to putter with inside plants or having to tend to the needs or inconvenience of pets, there was no greenery nor animals to clutter his pristine environment. He welcomed Sylvia into his home and had prepared an outside seating area on the back patio by his pool. A small patio table had been set with cups and plates for coffee and scones on this chilly afternoon get-together. The patio doors were open on all corners of the L-shaped living room kitchen area, and a cold breeze blew through the house. Escorting her out onto the patio, he pulled her chair out and seated her in a respectful manner at the two-seater table, almost as though he had played the scene out in his head before she had arrived.

He looked at Sylvia who was fidgeting in her seat and thought, *This is a failure and she sees right through me and my contrived attempt to please her.* Sylvia asked him about his deep-sea fishing, and he sighed with relief. Now having a subject to banter on about, he told her tales of the big one that got away. Self-interestedly going on about the topic, suddenly the roar of a motor interrupted the dialogue, and his voice was drowned out by his yardman turning the corner on a rider mower.

"I'm sorry, I'm so sorry," he shouted over the whir of the engine noise, I forgot that my yardman comes on Friday's." Joe continued to tell his story attempting to raise his voice over the sound of the mower. Sylvia felt sorry for him now. He appeared helpless and forlorn over his ruined attempt to impress her with a free-spirited and laid-back setting. "Let's go inside, I'm getting cold out here," Sylvia said, pulling her shawl sweater closed over her blouse. The afternoon wind had become brisk as the sun was setting, in keeping with the blunted end to their conversation.

Joe had always played a zero-sum game in business. Conversely, in his personal life, he wasn't willing to take the risk of either party losing. He was used to living alone and making his own rules. His hardwired and tactless nature was ruinous to an optimal introduction to a woman. At first, devoted to a newly acquired and irresistible female, the voluminous texts would flow forth as powerfully as the uncorking of a good bottle of wine.

Knowing he was odd in his ways, he usually found that most women gave way to his charming approach. Disappearing into the library for a few moments, Joe emerged with a handful of loose papers, scraps and notes all stacked together with a paperclip. "Do you mind if I read you some of my favorite quotes from books that I've read?" he asked softly.

He led her to two small chairs, covered in a petite flower print, explaining that these were not his taste. He had taken them off the hands of a neighbor who had taken ill and had moved away. Joe was a tall man and seemed to want to explain to his guest why his six-foot-four frame would have chosen to place those chairs in his home in a reading corner.

In the dim light of the table lamp, Joe began to read. Some of the quips in the books seemed to get a response from Sylvia. She was an avid reader and appeared to love that he not only had an appreciation for literature but additionally a romantic nature. Sylvia got up suddenly to use the bathroom, and when she returned, she let Joe know that although she had enjoyed their late afternoon time spent together, it was time for her to go.

Joe had created a CD for Sylvia to take home with her. She stood patiently in the doorway of his bedroom as he had gone in to retrieve the CD. "Oh wait, I want to list the names of the artists, so you'll know who you're listening to." She stood at the door patiently, watching him in silence. "OK, got it, let me walk you out." He rose from his knees where he had been crouched on the floor near his stereo— handing her the small gift he had taken the time to create for her.

In Joe's mind, Sylvia seemed to have enjoyed herself as she stepped into her car, the door ajar. Leaning on the door's window edge, he continued chatting and remarked that it had indeed gotten cold out. Sylvia again said, "Well, thank you for the afternoon." As he walked back up the brick walkway to his front door, he smiled pleased with himself.

Testimonies to her beauty, lusting and desirous came steadily over the next few days—he was inexorable in his free and wanton texts. Yet Joe was even more fascinated by his own visceral reactions and sexual response. His exhaustive narcissism would inevitably block the way to an authentic relationship. Perhaps that was all he ever wanted or indeed required, to examine his own psyche and masturbatory fantasies, finding comfort in his ability to get an erection at his age, despite his inadequate follow through.

Within the first week of getting to know Sylvia, Joe felt that he should tell her about a woman friend that he had known for the past four years. "I'm not dating anyone else right now, but I do have a best friend, a woman that I go to the movies with, out to dinner, and you know, shows and art festivals and such. There is nothing between us. We had once attempted to take the friendship there, well … you know, but I'm not into 'store boughts,' boobs that are bought, it's a real turn off to me."

He rattled on testifying to his purely platonic acquaintance with the woman. "I kind of feel sorry for her, she was raped you know, several times by different men." Sylvia, stunned by this revelation, paused and asked, "I'm sorry what did you just say?"

Joe repeated, "Yeah, it's true, she said she would go out with these men, drink too much, get sort of drunk, go home with them, and then the guys just took advantage of her." Sylvia could feel her blood pressure rising in her throat, the rush of anger flooding her chest and neck to a bright crimson pink. "How stupid are you to believe such nonsense? That woman didn't get raped! Rape is a severe issue, and I find it an insult to women everywhere when another woman uses that as some sort of badge...labeling herself as a victim when she is no more than a sex-addict attempting to make excuses for her more than promiscuous behavior.

"Well maybe you're right Joe said, running his hands through his dense wavy brown hair—twisting the ends between his fingers as if to punish himself for being such a gullible fool. He blurted out, "Well, maybe you're right, she did tell me that this one guy actually took her panties off while he was driving, and she was in the passenger seat and wearing jeans. I told her, how is that possible if you were wearing jeans? She said the guy was an absolute magician or something like that."

"Please stop, stop now, I can't bear to hear another word of this idiocy or my brain will simply bleed out of my ears!"

Why Joe had thought this information would be something that another woman would want to hear, qualified as one of the great mysteries of the world, never to be understood. Since Joe was only human, and as the saying goes, open mouth insert foot, Sylvia, a woman who prided herself on not being a jealous person, let the remark slide. Unbeknownst to Joe, however, she hadn't forgotten the conversation.

They got to know one another mostly over the phone having only been in each other's actual presence twice, and briefly at that. On the second date, Joe visited Sylvia's home. Listening to jazz and sipping wine the conversation went on for hours. Joe knew that she wasn't a woman to get involved physically without the emotional part in place first. This didn't stop him from pulling her close and kissing her hard and with intent on her perfectly shaped pink lips. "I just love your mouth, and the way you walk and move. Everything about you drives me crazy. I'm going to call you Slinky, Slinkster...how do you like your new nickname?"

With complete abandon, Joe texted her later that evening:

Joe: "God, I love your nipples...u r in trouble when we talk later. I want to be with you like there's no tomorrow! I can't stop thinking about you. I'm a crazy person for your body. Lord help me...do u like it that I desire you so? Do u skype for obvious reasons? To see you scantily clad tonight would thrill me. U will let me know what u like, but I think it will be clear."

Sylvia: "No, I don't skype...have a good night and sleep well."

Curt and to the point, Sylvia's text wasn't going to deter Joe from his conquest of her. The texts sprung forth with salacious requests, describing his fantasies and wild desire for her. Though she wouldn't engage in his illusory sexting-fest, she hadn't curtailed his behaviors either. There had been no admonishment from Sylvia. Joe had a habit of talking to himself while cleaning up around the house. He found himself asking, "Does this mean that she is accepting of my texts and she desires me in the same way?" In Joe's mind, no meant yes and his immodest, and unrestrained texts continued.

Unable to get her out of his thoughts, Joe texted Sylvia the next morning and asked to see her again at the end of the week. "Perhaps Thursday would work for you? I'd beg to see you sooner, but I have friends in from out of town for a few days. Some family members of my friend Susan. Her family is very much like my family. They have been good to me these past five years, including me in their holiday events. I thought I'd be a good guy and put them up for a few days, show them around town—you understand?" he said weakly.

Two weeks had gone by in silence. Joe's yearning for Sylvia's attention were obscured by his eventful days with his house guests. Home alone now, and with the quiet of the evening sinking in around him, he texted Sylvia.

The Texts:

Joe: "I remain full of hubris that you felt me so hard for you when last together...AND that you were excited."

Sylvia: "What do you want from me? It seems I am some blow-up fantasy doll in your mind. Your reticence to ask to see me, carnal texts, and lack of an invite

	to go on a proper date, are both insulting and confusing. The only conclusion I've come to is that you're either some closet pervert or a coward of sorts."
Joe:	"I hear you...although the imagery of you and wanting to cum on your chest doesn't endanger anyone. By the way, you should go to see the new French film that's out at the local university theater ASAP. It deals with sexual hunger and some off-center desires...it's a well-done film."
Sylvia:	"Yes, I should but I don't have a "friend" that I go to movies with, and theater and other casual stuff, and almost screw but don't!"
Sylvia:	"You have passed through my mind though sorry to see that all you wd wish for wd be to regurgitate your fantasies on me and in virtual reality only! Ur an odd guy. You should know that in the beginning my heart was in the right place with you. As Thomas Moore, the author of 'Care of the Soul' said, 'we're just two souls passing in the night...never recognizing the other and missing the opportunity to ever again join one another in this lifetime'.
Sylvia:	"I'd guess that you cd be bisexual or possibly gay tendencies. You seem more interested in your own erection than ever actually being with me in the flesh—sharing something together. 2nd possibility, you're afraid that you can't maintain an erection or please me—dunno."

Joe: "Interesting ish, bi/gay...never went down those avenues. Not all I wanted to do ...just bcoz there is no risk, exploding on your chest...many women love that, my experience anyway."

Joe: "I guess at the end of the day, I'm a sensual, hungry, artistic, shy, 35% selfish, insecure, sexually wound-up man-child who wants to b as condomlessly hard as that night... wd you take a rather sexy maybe transparent bra or no bra pic for me today or tmrw? Just asking ..."

EPILOGUE

*The cave you fear to enter holds the
treasure you seek.*

—Joseph Campbell

Man bashing and woman bashing can be heard almost anywhere nowadays. This is nothing new. It has been part of the common denominator of relationships between the sexes for centuries. At present, we are now faced with a more radical, powerful, and impactful change in the very base nature of the human relationship, and ultimately in how we meet our mates. We as humans have never encountered these social challenges before. Never in the history of mankind have the rituals of pairing off been so accessible.

One might think this a good thing. As a professional in the field of human sexuality, I do not. With the advent of computers and cutting-edge technology, a fast-paced society seems to have sprung up overnight into a new world. This is partly due to humans getting what they want instantaneously and because they know they can.

We have become a throwaway society. "Annoy us, look away when we're speaking to you, jump on board the bigger and better option because it's there and you can" has become the paradigm of our relational society today.

What we want is everywhere, and more and more of it is at a finger's touch away. Our material items can be ordered and delivered on our doorstep by the next day—and in some cases, the same day now, if we order early enough, in the breaking dawn hours of the morning. Why then are we dumbfounded when we find that our partner has found someone else to fulfill his or her needs and desires in the small lonely hours with the same instant gratification? Whether it's an old college friend or someone next door, or the candy-store maze of possibilities on the Internet, the next best thing (in your mind only) is right at your fingertips.

Within the technological advances of computer, smart phones and social media it seems that our "fast and quick" disposable society has ostensibly replaced committed relationships. In these past few decades, and especially now, great strides have been made regarding equality for women. With this equality comes a change in the traditional heterosexual relationship. Historically, men would assume the role of breadwinner, head of household, and a traditional "husband role" if they were the main income earner in the relationship.

This model of marriage/relationship has long gone by the wayside. This means that the woman is now expected to pull her own weight in the relationship, to participate as a partner, a working member of the team, bringing in a second income for the family.

Frequently this may not be an option in today's relationships if there are extenuating circumstances such as young children. The cost of daycare may outweigh the possible earnings of the spouse. But some remnants of those old-fashioned values and traditions of days gone by still exist. Viewing the relationship as a joint venture might be a better way of looking at a dedicated connection between two people today. I've often instructed my patients not to walk into a relationship with a fairy-tale mind-set that assumes all will be perfect without first looking at the MBV "mutual business venture" perspective.

This necessitates communication, compromise, dedication, financial transparency, and mutual present and future goals discussed beforehand. Fundamentally, a verbal contract of sorts between the two parties. Sounding a bit too mechanical and cold? No, not so. Not if one wants to avoid problems down the road. Knowing ahead of time where the couple stands on points and opinions of, finances, religion, children, geographical locations to live, sexuality, intimacy, friends, etc. are imperative.

Still, it seems to be all too easy now for couples to exist in a drive-up Burger King, drone delivery, instantaneous gratification-based society. Expecting something or someone immediately and precisely as they want. If it's not a perfect fit, return it postage paid the same day! In the past, regular folk (not movie stars) tended to stay in long-term marriages. Either they were too embarrassed to divorce, or the church looked down on it. For whatever reason, people tended to stick it out back then—perhaps for the sake of the children or convenience's sake.

No matter what day and age we live in, many aspects of relationship and human nature remains the same in most respects, from the beginning of time. Nature versus nurture? Specific traits are innate. We as *homo sapiens* may not be monogamous, but we are territorial. Wanting to belong to someone but not being owned by that person, jealousy, lack of trust or respect, a need to define oneself in the relationship, power and control ...all character traits still in existence today. '*The things we do to each other in the name of love*'.

That distinct, intangible magic between two people— will it ever be deciphered and filtered down to a specific science? The secret to those who make it in a lifetime-committed relationship and those who lose in love has been and always will be a puzzle, never to be truly understood as some arbitrary mandate or formula for the "perfect" relationship. It is not for me to judge or say who is right or wrong. However, in these testimonials of relatable human experiences, my own career experience and research, I have come to believe that love has shown itself not as something that one unassumingly wants, but rather an instinctive need.

I challenge the men and women brave enough to engage and involve themselves in a relationship to ask for equal dedication, respect, and commitment from their partners. Both sexes commit as many transgressions as their partners. There is no "better gender" among us. Our differences ultimately make us stronger, not weaker.

We as human beings want to be connected to another—to love and be loved. Those that profess otherwise have never truly loved.

—Dr. Arlene G. Krieger

The End

ACKNOWLEDGMENTS

This book could not have been written without the help of many. I wish to acknowledge the vast contributions others have made in illuminating my journey. Thank you to the professors, mentors, friends, and family who stood by my side throughout all academic endeavors. Warm thanks are also due to the many women, men, children, adolescents, and families whom I had the opportunity to encounter, and to those who invited me into their lives or whose lives I had the chance to touch.

Coming Spring 2020

Sex: From the Couch
THE SECOND COMING

FOR AN EXCERPT, TURN THE PAGE…

HERO

I'm a liar and a cheat and a coward, but I will never, ever, let a friend down. Unless of course not letting them down requires honesty, fair play, or bravery.

— *Mark Lawrence, Prince of Fools*

That attraction, that second glance that a firefighter, police officer, military man, or, for that matter, any man in uniform can command is the stereotype of a woman swooning over the tall, handsome "white knight" in shining armor—coming to the rescue of those in need.

Johnny was a specific breed of firefighter. Thirty years of service and he had retired while still in good health. Amelia's friends would later ask her, "Really? What on earth were you thinking? Was it the muscles and six-pack? Where has your brain gone girl?!"

It was the summer and hurricane season, and all eyes were on the local news and weather channels; a storm warning was issued, and the mad rush was on for water, gas, and supplies. Amelia's brothers had insisted that she caravan up to Atlanta with them, but she had large dogs and the veterinarian kennel was already full. Having previously braved out possible hurricanes and those that had turned into monsters, this one wasn't going to send her running. Besides, her new guy had insisted on staying over with her while awaiting the storm, or as the weather forecasters called it, the impending tropical depression.

She had met Johnny a few weeks earlier when out in the country at a well-known harvest market, open only a few months out of the year with lines so long you'd think you were in line for the newly discovered gold rush.

One could die an early and blissful death stuffed from their baked goods, especially the sticky, gooey goodness of those more than memorable cinnamon buns and strawberry shakes! Amelia had always loved to ride out to the berry farm ever since she was a child.

He was standing to the left of her with numerous children by his side, all calling for "shakes...shakes...shakes."

She couldn't help but notice, and without a second thought she joined in their conversation. "I see that these babies have found the secret to great happiness and long lives. Are you their 'pied piper.?'

He was quick to reply, "No ma'am I am their grandfather!"

"Their grandfather? Why there are twelve kids here... are they all yours? Well Ma'am, yes indeed they are. I've got twenty-two grandkids.

Laughing, Amelia blurted out, "Well then, you must be keeping this place in business for the past thirty or so years!"

Looking back on the innocence of how they had first met, Amelia could never find a reason to blame herself for what was to be uncovered months later.

She and Johnny went out that weekend, and it was "on" after that first date. He would drive into town on a Friday night, and then head back home to Ocala where he raised alpacas as a tax deduction for the country farm he had inherited from his grandfather. The drive was an hour away for him, yet he headed back up to Amelia devoting the rest of the weekend to her until early Monday morning.

A bit of a crazy figure eight rendezvous, hours of back and forth road time, but what the heck Johnny thought, "We're in love."

She had experienced that kind of mutual slam-bang attraction with a man once before. Chemistry is always exciting in the beginning yet something to be wary of when it starts out with a bang. In her past experiences with men, that hot attraction often leads to disappointment. This man with the great personality would be more like a visit to Dante's Inferno.

Johnny had insisted on staying with Amelia during the hurricane. Her friends told her she was crazy. "Why you don't even really know this man," Halle said in a

reprimanding tone. Having been her best friend and con-
fidant for the past ten years, Halle felt a responsibility to
speak her truth when it came to men, all men, no matter
who was dating them.

"But he is a loving father and grandfather of loads of
kids," Amelia said laughing out loud.

The weather was getting worse, and although Johnny
had assured her that he was coming up to help her with
the storm shutters, it was getting late and she had not
heard back from him by late that afternoon. He had called
her in the morning on his way to the Keys, saying that he
had to pick up some lobster traps from his ex-girlfriend's
house or she was going to throw them out. It seemed a bit
odd, but heck, what did she know about lobster traps. She
thought, *Oh well, maybe the things are expensive.*

The handymen that usually did work for the family
were at her mother's house across town. Beginning to
worry that she'd be on her own for this storm, she called
and found they were just finishing up over there. "Of
course, Ms. Amelia, of course, we will be over to help you."
She hung up the phone breathing a sigh of relief.

Before dusk, Johnny called saying he was finally on his
way back. "Oh well, I sorta got caught up helping her and
some friends put up her shutters on the second-floor windows. I'm headed your way and should be there in an hour
or so...no worries. I'll work into the night if necessary."

"It's OK Amelia stated calmly; I've taken care of it."

The storm wailed outside the hurricane-shuttered
windows. The powerful gusts slammed the metal shutters

against the window frames with such force that she thought they would perish. They huddled together in the safety of the secured living room, watching the weather and storm surge flood reports until finally the power went out. She was sure they were going to drown, even if the roof didn't blow off.

While clinging on to Johnny, both curled up in each other's arms and burrowed into the large oversized sofa cushions, Amelia asked desperately, "Is there a chance that we're going to drown? Are you sure we're not in a flood zone? The National Hurricane Center said this could be a level five, and all the neighbors have evacuated. It's pitch black out there and everyone has evacuated—are we going to die tonight, Johnny?"

Made in the USA
Columbia, SC
19 March 2020

89565792R00121